P9-EEN-211

All in a Day

All in a Day

Alexis Nicole

www.urbanbooks.net

Urban Books, LLC
97 N18th Street
Wyandanch, NY 11798

All in a Day Copyright © 2013 Alexis Nicole

All rights reserved. No part of this book may be repro-
duced in any form or by any means without prior consent
of the Publisher, except brief quotes used in reviews.

ISBN 13: 978-1-60162-397-3
ISBN 10: 1-60162-397-6

First Trade Paperback Printing December 2013
Printed in the United States of America

10 9 8 7 6 5 4 3 2 1

*This is a work of fiction. Any references or similarities
to actual events, real people, living or dead, or to real
locales are intended to give the novel a sense of reality.
Any similarity in other names, characters, places, and
incidents is entirely coincidental.*

Distributed by Kensington Publishing Corp.
Submit Wholesale Orders to:
Kensington Publishing Corp.
C/O Penguin Group (USA) Inc.
Attention: Order Processing
405 Murray Hill Parkway
East Rutherford, NJ 07073-2316
Phone: 1-800-526-0275
Fax: 1-800-227-9604

To the Cannon-Hampton family.
Thank you for the inspiration.

And

To Lillian and David Cannon. Thank you for being a wonderful example. God Bless your 60 years of marriage.

Chapter 1

Morgan

My mother's favorite phrase was "God never makes mistakes." Even to this day, that saying drove me nuts. He may not make mistakes but He certainly loves to play jokes on people. The first seventeen years of my life were definitely proof of that. Any God who would put me in the family that I had, growing up in middle-of-nowhere Georgia where the townspeople were nosier than the FBI, CIA, and black mothers combined is one hell of a comedian. *Well played, God.* For the last eight years I had tried to free myself from the tyranny that was my childhood, but this conversation was bringing back all the bad memories.

"Oh, you were so adorable. All the mothers were so jealous." Even over the phone I could tell my mother was doing her ritual walk down memory lane.

"Mom, did you pull out the photo albums?"

"I can't help it. They're the only things I have since you're all the way across the world."

I could hear the pain in my mother's voice. Leaving Georgia was always my main mission in life. If there was a law permitting children to live on their own, I probably would have left the first time my mother signed me up for a beauty pageant. Unfortunately, I had to wait until college to make my great escape.

"Ma, London is only like an eight-hour flight from Georgia." I was trying my best to change the subject. My mother loved putting the guilt trip on me. "You and Daddy can come visit anytime."

"You know how your father feels about flying." She said it like I should have known that wasn't an option. "Oh, Morgan, I just found the picture of you when you qualified to compete for Miss Teen Georgia. I will never know how you lost to Sue Baker. You were the best thing on that stage."

As my mother rambled on about my glory days, I couldn't help but think about that competition, when I consciously made a decision to lose.

Winning Miss Teen Georgia meant possibly going on to Miss Teen USA and I refused to be a part of that. Sue Baker was a sweet girl from Athens who I competed against a few times before. Her strawberry-blond hair, blue eyes, and girl-next-door persona was definitely heavy competition for the other girls, but the certain tricks of the trade that I possessed couldn't be beat.

"Okay, Miss Morgan Willis, how are you doing it?" she asked as we changed our hair and makeup for the next segment of the competition.

"Doing what?"

"Making those judges drool all over you. I can't even get judge number three to look at me." She paused and studied me in the mirror for a second.

As I continued to curl and pin my hair, I could tell she was searching for some sort of magical answer.

"You're sleeping with one of them, aren't you?" she asked as if she came to a revelation.

All I could do was laugh in her face at that ridiculous suggestion. "Sue, trust me. This competition does not mean that much to me."

"Well, it means everything to me."

I could see the disappointment in her eyes as she tried to pull herself together to finish changing into her next outfit. Pageants were just something I did to please my mother and rack up the scholarship cash so I could get out of this godforsaken state. I never realized that these things actually meant something to these girls. Sue was such a sweet girl and I felt bad that I didn't have the same passion for pageants as she did.

For the next twenty minutes I gave Sue the Morgan Crash Course to winning pageants. I shared all the little secrets I'd learned over the years, and even the scoop on the judges on the panel. With Sue having the goods and me doing the complete opposite of everything I knew, she went on to win the title and I never did another pageant again.

"I still think that crown should have been yours," my mother continued to gripe.

"Mom, enough about me. How's everything at home?" I had to get this conversation moving elsewhere.

"Same ol', same ol'. Just trying to tie up all the loose ends of this reunion, which everyone is hoping you will attend this time."

The Maxson family reunion was my mother's favorite pastime. She was the youngest of six children, but seemed to be the most responsible one, which meant she always planned the biannual event. My mom felt like it was a time for the whole family to get together and catch up. I just saw it as everybody being able to get in your business all at once. I hadn't been to a reunion since I left for college.

"Mom, I don't think I'll be able to. I have so much going on with work, and Ahvi has been in and out of town lately."

"Speaking of Ahvi, when are we going to meet this mystery man?"

"Soon."

That was a lie. I was totally and completely in love with Ahvi. We'd been together over a year, living together for six months, and I was the happiest I'd ever been in my life. I didn't think I'd ever met anyone so wonderful, but I wasn't ready to do the whole meet-the-family thing.

"Well, you've been dating this person for a while and you have yet to introduce him to your mother. If you ask me it doesn't seem like you guys are serious."

I didn't ask. "We are serious."

"You couldn't be if your parents don't know him."

"Mom, we're engaged. It's serious."

There it was, like word vomit. I had absolutely no intention of telling my mother about my engagement, but her prying just made me give in. I waited what seemed like an eternity for my mother's response. If I knew Juanita Willis, she was furious.

"Engaged?"

"Yes, ma'am," I said as if I were twelve years old again. *Lord, please let her be gentle.*

"This is so wonderful."

I knew she was going to be . . . Wait. What? Did she just say it was wonderful? Okay, who is this woman and what has she done with my mother? A minute ago she was complaining that she never met Ahvi and now she's excited that I'm engaged? Am I the only one confused here?

"You are actually happy I'm engaged?"

"Absolutely, and I think you should have the wedding here in Georgia during the family reunion."

Okay, now I know she's trippin'. I want a beautiful, small ceremony in Spain or Paris, not some barnyard hoedown in Macon, Georgia. I had to get out of this.

"Mom, the reunion is two weeks away. That is not enough time to do anything for a wedding."

"Of course it is. We'll do it at the church, everyone will already be here, and the family banquet will be the reception."

The family banquet will be my wedding reception? Is she serious? What has this turned into? If I could take anything back in my life, the words "I'm engaged" would definitely be on the top of the list.

"Mom, I really don't think—"

"Morgan Anne Willis, you have been away from home for eight years and you have never really included your father and me in any major decisions of your life. I will not miss my only child's wedding. You are getting married in Georgia. Now that's it."

I debated a lot of things with my mother, but when she said "that's it," that was it. No ifs, ands, or buts about it. So there it was. In two weeks I was going to be faced with my worst nightmare. The Lord just kept getting funnier by the moment.

"Yes, ma'am." Those were the only words I could counter with.

"Great. You find your tickets and I'll handle everything else. Love you, baby. Bye."

Just like that she was gone, leaving me speechless, still holding the phone to my ear until that annoying busy tone started beeping. What in the hell had just happened? How did I end up having my wedding in Georgia—in two weeks? I began pacing the floors trying to come up with a plan to get out of what could possibly be a total disaster of a wedding. *Maybe I can call my mama back and just tell her we are not coming. What can she do, spank me? No, that won't work. She's probably already picking out flower arrangements.*

"Darling, I'm not criticizing your methods, but if you plan on putting a hole in our floor maybe I should go out and buy a rug."

The thick British accent startled me as Ahvi walked through the door. For a brief moment, I completely forgot about what just transpired and rushed into my love's arms to plant the biggest kiss I could on Ahvi's lips.

"You're home early. How was Paris?"

"Oh, Paris is Paris. I lived in a conference room for three days."

Ahvi was brilliant in international business and had become a junior partner in a big firm here in London. Who knew that meeting someone in a pub would lead to such an amazing love? I was so happy to be spending the rest of my life with this beautiful soul, but I didn't want to start it off in Georgia.

"My love, we need to talk." I led Ahvi to the couch to reveal my mother's plans for our wedding. I was hoping that I would, at least, have my fiancé on my side and we would decide to absolutely not go.

"If you're going to tell me you're leaving me, I'm keeping the flat."

"Of course I'm not leaving you and we would sell the apartment if I did, but my news isn't good." I took a breath and prepared to speak as fast as I could. "I sort of told my mom about our engagement and now she wants to throw us a wedding in Georgia in two weeks." I closed my eyes and waited for that glorious sound of outrage.

"Oh, darling, that's wonderful," Ahvi said in delight.

Okay, seriously. What the hell is going on? First my mother, now my fiancé. I must've stepped into the Twilight Zone.

"Honey, you do realize this is going to be in the backwoods of Georgia . . . in two weeks . . . during my family's reunion."

"I understand that, love, but I think it's time for me to finally meet your family."

What was I hearing? This was not the plan. We were supposed to have a quaint little wedding in Spain, my family not included, and that would be it. This was not happening.

"But—"

"I know you have concerns, but let's go and do this for your family and we'll come back and have the wedding we planned."

Ahvi gently kissed me on my forehead and then disappeared to our bedroom. So, just like that I was outvoted. How did my life go from a dream to my worst nightmare in an hour? *Well played, God . . . well played.*

Chapter 2

Janette

If I never heard the name Morgan Willis again it would be too soon. My whole life I'd been compared to my pageant queen cousin. "Morgan's so pretty. Morgan's so talented." I was starting to feel like the Jan Brady of the family. It was bad enough that everyone in town loved her, but her being extremely close to my daddy I'd always hated. He called her his favorite niece and he always doted on her. He even helped pay for all those pageants she was in. The most my father did for me was teach me how to fix a carburetor. The day she left for college was the day I began making people forget about Morgan Willis.

Living in her shadow the rest of my life was not on my agenda. I transformed my style from tomboy to bombshell, I owned the biggest boutique in Macon with my best friend Millie, and I even had an amazing boyfriend. Well, he wasn't officially mine, yet, but he would be. Things were perfect and this upcoming family reunion was the perfect place to show off just how perfect my life was.

"'Scuse me. Do you have this in black?" a heavyset woman with rainbow color hair said, interrupting my thoughts. She held up a tangerine halter dress that looked ten sizes too small for her. "I like this for the club but black is more slimming."

So is Weight Watchers but I guess you can't wear that to the club.

"I think we're all out of the black," I said through a fake smile.

She held the dress up to her body and stepped back from the counter. She examined it from head to toe and even twirled in it to get the full effect. "You think this color match my skin?"

I think it matches your hair.

"I think you gon' shut the club down with that dress, girl." No fake smile needed for that comment. The thought of her going to the club in this tangerine halter dress that probably couldn't fit her left arm made me chuckle. As long as she was buying, I was selling, regardless of how she looked.

She squealed with delight and went back to the racks for more.

"It is hotter than a slave ship out there," Millie griped as she came through the door.

Millie Parker and I had been friends since grade school. Everybody referred to her as the Mouth of the South. She knew everybody's business and wasn't afraid to tell anybody who would listen. Being friends with Millie had its advantages and disadvantages, but she beat up Marlene Dade for me in the fourth grade for calling me a jiggaboo and I'd been loyal to her ever since.

"Maybe if you would have gotten here at nine when it was still cool you wouldn't be complaining."

"If I would have gotten here at nine, I wouldn't have so much dirt for you."

I hated when Millie strolled in here whenever she felt like it, especially when I was dealing with costumers by myself, but good gossip always made me forgive and forget. Millie came behind the register and took a seat in what I called her spilling-the-tea chair. Hearing other people's business from Millie was almost like an event.

"Okay, so you remember Ms. Tucker who used to run the nursery?"

"Yeah." I was getting excited.

"How 'bout she's been boosting electronics and selling them out of her back room?" Millie said it like she had struck gold.

"That's it? She's been doing that for years."

"Really?"

"Where you think my daddy got that forty-two-inch TV from?"

Millie looked slightly offended that she hadn't known about this sooner. She quickly recovered and proceeded with the rest of her news. "Well, did you know Mrs. Johnson from New Mount Zion Baptist was sleeping with their pastor, Reverend Dixon?"

"And First Lady Dixon is sleeping with Mrs. Johnson's nephew," I countered with additional information.

"Are you serious?" Millie was in complete shock.

"All those trips up to Morehouse ain't for speaking engagements."

Millie looked so hurt. My best friend was slippin'. She'd never been this late with gossip before. I guessed all that time she'd been spending with her new boyfriend, Ray, had her worried about her own business now. This lack of juice just made me mad that she was late all over again.

"Damn. Well, I guess you know about Morgan's wedding, too, then."

Okay, now I was shocked. For eight years it was all quiet on the Morgan front and now all of a sudden she's getting married. "Where did you hear that?"

"I ran into your aunt Juanita and she gave me this 'save the date' flier." She pulled a small square piece of paper out of her purse and I snatched it out of her hand before she could even read it to me.

"Beanie gave you this?" I asked, still scanning the flier.

"Yeah, she's passing them out to everyone. She seems really excited about it."

I read each word on that paper carefully as if it were a golden ticket. I could feel myself getting hot as I registered what was actually happening.

"She's getting married at the family reunion?" I hadn't realized my voice went up two octaves and I was almost yelling.

"So I'm guessing you didn't know about this. Yes! Still got it." Millie seemed delighted with herself that she finally gave me news that I didn't know about.

This is not happening. All that effort and hard work I put in to get everyone past the Morgan era now is about to be completely ruined. It's bad enough that she's coming back into town, but a wedding? It's gonna be the twenty-four-seven Morgan channel.

"How is it even possible to pull off a wedding in two weeks?"

"You know your aunt can move mountains, especially when it comes to Morgan."

I loved my best friend, but she could not take a hint when it came to rhetorical questions. *I have to do something about this. I refuse to let Miss Perfect come back and destroy everything I built just because she got somebody to say "I do."* I quickly grabbed my things and headed for the door.

"Where are you going?"

"My folks' house. Hold it down while I'm gone."

I couldn't make that twenty-five-minute drive from the boutique to my parents' house fast enough. I continually tried to play out scenarios in my mind to prevent this thing from happening. *She can get married anywhere. Why does it have to be here and why right now? Europe isn't good enough for the queen? Must be too many already there for her to compete.*

I pulled up to my parents' house and quickly hopped out. I ran up the porch so fast I almost broke my neck skipping the steps. "Ma? Dad?" I called out from the front door.

"We're in the kitchen, Nettie."

I could hear loud bursts of laughter as I walked through the house. Was it happening already? Were people laughing at me? This situation was not good for my psyche. I was becoming paranoid already. I walked in the kitchen to find my parents, my brother, and my aunt Juanita at the table.

"Hey, honey. I thought you would be at the shop today." My mother didn't even bother to give me a hug to greet me.

"I left early. What's going on in here?" Like I didn't already know the answer.

"Beanie came over to tell us the news about Morgan," my father answered with a huge grin on his face. His eyes were lit up like a Christmas tree.

"Yeah, I heard. I'm sad I'm the last to know. We were so close." I tried my best not to throw up after that statement. This whole situation was a dagger to my heart.

"I'm sorry, baby." My aunt finally got up from the table and embraced me. It was so genuine until she slapped into my hand that small piece of paper that brought my whole world down. "I'm just so excited to get the word out. Now we don't have much time so I'm going to need all the help I can get."

Before I could utterly object to what she was suggesting, my father interjected, "Nettie would be happy to help. Anything for you and baby girl."

I hated that my father called Morgan "baby girl." Ever since I could remember that had always been his nickname for her. She was his baby girl and he was her uncle Bug, short for Junebug, which was the name everyone else called him. It all made me sick.

"Actually I have a lot going on with the boutique and all, so I don't think—"

"Nonsense," my father cut me off again. "Now this is blood. You plan on attending that reunion; then you plan on helping with this wedding." My father's voice was stern and I knew not to challenge him. He had said his peace and that was it.

"Great. We'll get started tomorrow." Beanie kissed everyone good-bye and headed out the back door.

"Wow. Baby girl gettin' married, and here in Georgia."

My father continued to beam and it made me sick to my stomach. Without even speaking another word, I left the kitchen and raced to my old room. Not only did I have to endure this wedding, now I had to help with it, too. At this point all I could do was lie across my bed and cry. *Lord, let this be as painless as possible.*

Chapter 3

Henry

Growing up, I always thought the National Football League would be my place of employment. I never had another dream for myself. I was four years old when my daddy put a football in my hands and told me that if I worked hard enough, I could be a force to be reckoned with. Ever since then I'd been focused on playing football, the money that came with playing football, and the women who came with the money. It's funny how you had a plan for your life, and sometimes God had a completely different plan. I never in a million years thought that, instead of being a wide receiver for an NFL team, I would own my own car service business. The Lord seemed to have a twisted sense of humor.

"That'll be perfect, Don. I'll see you in a few days." I hung up with a business investor I had been working with for a few months. Don Perkins had business ventures in all of the hottest spots in the country: Miami, Atlanta, New York, and Los Angeles. Now he was interested in doing business with me, and I was definitely ready for anything that made me more money.

I got up from my desk and headed out to the lot where all my employees were preparing their cars for the day. It was a beautiful sight to see that I went from one old-school Cadillac my grandfather gave me after graduating high school that I would use to drive my homeboys places, charging them gas money, to now having over thirty cars, limos, and SUVs. Business was booming and it was only about to get better.

I spotted Beau washing and waxing the Lincoln Town Car he was working in for the day and made my way over to him. Beau and I had been friends from the womb. Our mothers were really close growing up, so when they got pregnant around the same time it was almost inevitable for us to be friends. I had no problems with giving him a job to try to keep him out of the usual trouble that he got in.

"'All the world's a stage,' my brother. 'And all the men and women merely players,'" I said as I dapped him up. "And, I plan on getting an Oscar."

"What the hell you talkin' about, bruh?" Beau put a rag in the back pocket of his jumpsuit and proceeded around the car to continue to clean the other side.

"I'm talking about opportunities. Don Perkins is interested in investing in yours truly, Mr. Henry Lloyd, and expanding my company to luxury rentals." I was grinning like the Cheshire cat, but Beau looked confused.

"Okay. What does that mean?"

"It means that rich and/or famous people who come into town who don't want to be driven around can have the option in renting luxury vehicles like Porches, Bentleys, Mercedes, et cetera. Bruh, this could mean triple the profits."

I could see the wheels turning in Beau's head. I wasn't completely sure if he understood what I was saying or trying to figure out if it was a good venture. Beau was only a driver for me, but I always came to him when new things in the company presented themselves. I wanted him to be a partner but he didn't have the money or the will to sit behind a desk all day. This was my way of keeping him involved on the business side.

"It sounds good, but ain't no rich and/or famous person gonna be down here in Macon driving no Bentley."

"We're going to start in Atlanta. I have a meeting with Don up there in a few days."

Beau became silent again and continued to wipe down the car. I wasn't expecting for him to be extremely excited but I was kind of hoping for some more feedback. It was unlike him to not have anything to say.

"Well, that sounds like what's up. Just make sure I can hold one of them cars from time to time. So I can go to the club and straight stunt on 'em."

I chuckled at the thought of Beau's big, tall, lanky self pulling up to the club in a $150,000 vehicle when everyone knew he drove limos for a living.

"Speaking of cars, when you gon' let me work the Escalade? I'm not gettin' no play in this Lincoln." Beau threw the rag he was working with on top of the hood. He looked at the car like it was his mortal enemy but could never win battles against it. He was a good driver but he did seem to get distracted by the women he was trying to impress, which didn't take much effort on his part. The women around here seemed to be impressed by the minor things, so I could understand why the Cadillac would be a better look for his game.

"Everybody starts in the Lincoln during their probation period. You know that."

"Whatever, man." He chuckled. His mood immediately switched and I could tell something was wrong. "Ay, you think I could holla at you in your office?"

I had no idea what was going on, but it couldn't be good. Beau usually never wanted to speak to me in private unless he needed something or got into something he shouldn't have. I nodded my head and he followed me off the lot. I was preparing myself for whatever he was about to say to me, but I was hoping it had nothing to do with the law. I couldn't afford to lose him at work.

When we got to my office I quickly took a seat before he could say anything. I knew any news from Beau had to be taken in a seated position. When he began pacing back and forth I was assured that it definitely wasn't good.

"I'm not sure how to tell you this," he began.

He was taking his time trying to strategize what he had to say, but I really didn't have time for all the suspense. "Look, B, if this got something to do with legal issues I don't know if I can help this time."

Beau stopped pacing and looked at me as if he was disappointed that just came out my mouth. I didn't mean to offend him, but it was no secret that he and the police didn't get along.

"Naw, man, this ain't got nothing to do with me."

"Oh, well, then spit it out." I started shoveling through the papers on my desk because if this news didn't have to do with him going to jail, I could multitask.

"Morgan's coming back to town to get married."

It was like the world stopped spinning. I couldn't move. I couldn't breathe. I just stared at the papers in my hand. I needed to gather my thoughts and quickly. I couldn't look like a simp in front of my boy, but Morgan was the only girl I ever loved and the only one who broke my heart. I couldn't believe she would just pop up out of nowhere after eight years to get married.

"When did you hear that?" I finally asked but couldn't bring myself to look at Beau.

"This morning. I ran into my aunt Beanie when I was leaving from Treece's apartment. I thought she was gonna bust me out about that 'cause I did have the walk-of-shame swag on. You know Treece is a freak."

Is this fool serious? He is over here discussing his sex life and my personal life just got turned upside down. I couldn't care less about what he and his random freak did.

"Anyway, all she did was tell me how excited she was and handed me this flier." Beau pulled a small square paper out of his pocket and handed it to me. He finally took a seat in one of the chairs in front of my desk. He had a look of accomplishment on his face, like he successfully completed a mission. I guessed he felt like the hard part was over; now he could relax.

I read over the paper carefully and tried to comprehend what was happening. I honestly didn't know how to feel right now. I'd tried for years to forget about this girl, but every time I thought I'd succeeded memories came flooding back.

"Good for her," I finally said. I tried to have a nonchalant tone.

"Word? You're cool with this?" Beau seemed surprised at the approach I took.

I had to admit I was a little shocked myself. "Why wouldn't I be?" I responded, keeping my composure. One thing I'd learned from running my own business was to always keep a poker face.

"I just thought since you two were—"

"When's your first pickup?" I cut Beau off.

"Not until one-thirty."

I could tell he was extremely confused, which was what I needed him to be right now. If I told him too much he would probably try to talk me out of it, and I just wanted him to follow my lead.

"Good. Let's make a run real quick."

I got up from my desk and headed toward my car. Beau reluctantly followed me in silence. We'd known each other long enough to know when not to ask questions. I was glad he knew that this was one of those times.

About ten minutes into the drive I peeped over at Beau to see if he was catching on to where we were going. He seemed a little uneasy about what was happening. I didn't want to put him in an awkward position, but I had to see about this engagement myself. I pulled up to the Willis house and we both took deep breaths.

"Bruh, I'm not sure what you're doing, but we can go back to the lot right now," he said, hesitating to take off his seat belt.

"Just follow my lead." I hopped out the car and headed up to the porch, which I had done so many times before. I remembered taking Morgan out on our first date. This walk through the driveway had me so nervous the petals of the flowers I held in my hand were shivering. All I kept imagining was her daddy coming to the front door with a shotgun. I had that same nervous feeling in the pit of my stomach as I knocked on the door. Beau stood on the steps behind me, allowing me to take the lead as I had requested.

"Well, what a surprise," Mrs. Willis said as she opened the door. She gave me a hug and a kiss on the cheek and ushered us into the house.

"I hope we didn't catch you at a bad time. Beau and I were just in the neighborhood and wanted to stop by and holla at you for a second." I saw in my peripheral vision Beau cutting his eyes at me. I didn't bother to look over at him to counteract his look. I grinned at Mrs. Willis and sat down on one of the couches in the living room.

"Oh naw, you're fine. Just about to start setting up appointments for Morgan when she gets into town."

"Yeah, I heard the good news. Congratulations."

"Well, thank you, Henry. I'm just interested to finally meet this fiancé of hers."

I tried my best to maintain a straight face, but I could feel myself becoming transparent. Even after all these years, it was difficult for me to sit here and hear about Morgan's fiancé, who wasn't me.

"Oh, I'm sorry. I—"

"No need to apologize." I cut her off before she could get into the whole sympathy rampage. "We actually came over here to see when they were coming into town."

"We did?" Beau blurted out from his seat. Mrs. Willis and I both looked at him at the same time. "I mean, we did," he finally agreed after he read my eyes.

"Well, I don't think she's made any arrangements just yet, but I'm sure it'll be in a couple of days."

"When you do get that information, Beau would be more than happy to pick her up free of charge." At this point I was free-styling it, but I had a mini plan forming.

"I would?" Beau blurted out again.

I swear if I was three feet closer to him I would smack the living daylights out the back of his head.

"I mean, of course I would, Aunt Beanie. That's fam."

"Oh no, I couldn't ask y'all to do that. Besides, Earl and I haven't seen her in so long. We want to be the ones to pick her up."

I could tell this suggestion would die quickly if I didn't come up with something and fast. I wanted to be able to speak to Morgan alone before she made any more moves toward this marriage thing, and I knew once the family was around I would never get that opportunity. I definitely needed an audible, something that could distract Mrs. Willis without feeling guilty about not picking Morgan up from the airport.

"You know what she would love? A welcome home party." *Damn, I am good.* "I mean, after being away from home for eight years, she needs something to show how much she's been missed."

"Now that's a dope idea, Aunt Beanie. You could cook all her favorite foods she probably ain't have over there in Europe," Beau said, finally getting on board. I didn't know if he was saying this for me, Morgan, or because he just wanted free food.

"Exactly," I chimed back in. "Besides, I have a couple of meetings in Atlanta later on in the week. I can have Beau drive me and then pick her up whenever she gets in."

I felt like this argument was pretty convincing, but Mrs. Willis's silence was giving me doubts. I knew how much she loved Morgan, so the idea of giving a party in her honor would definitely be something she would jump at.

"Okay," she finally said. "But you tell my baby nothing about it and you bring her right to me."

I tried to contain the ear-to-ear grin that I could feel forming across my face. This might be my only shot and I was happy to have an opportunity to take it.

"Well, we really should be getting back to work." I stood from the couch and gave Mrs. Willis a bear hug and a kiss on the cheek. "Just call Beau with the details."

Beau followed suit with embracing her and we both made our way back to the car. I had a sense of accomplishment in my glide. I honestly had no idea what I was actually doing, but for some reason it felt good.

"What the hell was that?" Beau asked once we were in the car.

"Strategy, my dude. Pure strategy." I put the key in the ignition and drove back to the lot. Wedding or not, things were about to get real interesting.

Chapter 4

Morgan

How Ahvi got tickets so quickly I would never know, but here I was four days after the worst phone call of my life, heading to the airport. I was dreading every bit of this trip. I would have loved to just go, have no one ask me any questions, get this ceremony over with and head back home, but knowing the Maxson family that was not going to be possible. This was about to be a complete disaster. To make it worse, Ahvi still had business to handle so I was doing this first leg alone.

"Are you positive you can't go with me now?" I held on to my fiancé tight, still trying to convince Ahvi that taking off work was a good idea.

"I'm positive, darling, but I promise I'll be there a few days before the wedding."

This was so agonizing. I tried to give Ahvi my best sad face one more time but it wasn't working.

"Everything will be okay. I promise."

"You don't know these people. This is not going to be a smooth trip."

"Well they raised you, so they can't be that bad."

As comforting as that was, I was still having a hard time with this. I hadn't dealt with my family in eight years and going back to Georgia under these circumstances was very unsettling. As the taxi pulled up to the airport I realized it was too late to back out now. I hugged and kissed Ahvi as passionately as I could. As much as we worked, we'd never been this far apart from each other for this long.

"I promise everything will be fine. And I'll be there before you know it," Ahvi reassured me after coming up for air.

"If you say so." We kissed a final time and I headed into the airport.

From the time I left Ahvi's side until the time I landed in Atlanta was a complete blur. The last thing I remembered was telling the first-class flight attendant to provide me with lots of vodka. I guessed she gave me enough to knock me out because I was now stepping into the sweltering heat of good ol' Georgia. Atlanta's airport traffic was always busy, so I tried to maneuver around to see if I could see my parents' car.

"Ay, what up, kinfolk?" I heard a voice yell from a distance. I looked around to see exactly who this ignorant fool was talking to. There's nothing like being back in Georgia and running into ratchet black people.

"Yo, Morgan." The voice yelled out again. My heart dropped when I realized it was for me. I spotted a tall, slender, chocolate man in an all-black suit with a driver's hat on, standing at the passenger side of a Lincoln Town Car. At first I didn't recognize him, until he flashed his smile.

"Beau?" I said as I finally got close to him.

"The one and only. Man, cousin, give me a hug." He pulled me close to him and squeezed the life out of me. Beau was the youngest of my aunt Melba's children. Growing up, we all thought he would go into the NBA because no one could beat him on the court, but the judicial court kept beating him. He stayed in and out of juvie, which eventually messed up his college scholarship.

"Man, cuz, you look better than a bowl of cheese grits," he said as he finally let me go. "And just as thick, too."

"Thanks, I guess. Where's my folks? I thought they would be picking me up."

"Well, Uncle Earl is working a double at the garage and Aunt Beanie is planning a surprise for you, so they asked me to pick you up."

I was sad and relieved at the same time. As much as I didn't want to be back, I did kind of wish my parents would have been the first faces I saw.

"Thanks, Beau, but you didn't have to get all dressed up for me."

"Oh naw, this is my uniform. I'm a chauffeur." Beau proudly tugged on his tie and grinned from ear to ear. As hot as it was out here I knew he was dying, but I was glad to see him happy and out of trouble. "Now get in this car before them boys give me a ticket."

He grabbed my bag from my hand and proceeded to put it in the trunk. I quickly hopped in the back seat like I was instructed, only to be immediately startled by the man who was already in the seat next me. "You okay?" he said.

I caught my breath and tried to slow my heartbeat. As I shook my head yes, I took in the sight that was beside me. His tall, muscular build was noticeable even through his suit. His milk-chocolate skin was still as smooth as I remembered. And the peach fuzz that I used to despise was now a full-grown goatee that framed his full lips and beautifully bright smile. This was a face I could never forget. Our whole high school career we were seemingly attached to the hip. He was the football star, I was the pageant princess, and everyone thought we were going to get married. I thought at some point we even believed the hype.

"Welcome home, babe." He handed me a single white rose and kissed me softly on my cheek.

"Hello, Henry. What are you doing here?"

"I wanted to make sure you got home okay."

"And you couldn't have called the house later to find that out? I know you still have the number."

"I could've, but what fun is that?"

I couldn't believe this. I'd only been in town fifteen minutes and I'd already accumulated a headache. *Maybe I can catch a flight back to London if I get out of the car right now and run for it.*

"Y'all ready?" Beau hopped in the driver seat and took off before I could say anything. I should have known something was up. Beau and Henry had been friends since the womb. Their mothers were friends since high school and were excited when they became pregnant at the same time. My parents probably never asked them to pick me up; one of these idiots probably volunteered.

"Seriously, Morgan, it is really good to see you. We've missed you around here," Henry continued.

"We?" I had known Henry a long time, and even though we hadn't spoken in years I knew when he was up to something.

"Well, me in particular."

Told you he was up to something.

"You know I'm here to get married, right?" Henry was my past and I had to remind him that I had a present and a future that didn't include him.

"Ay, I've been meaning to ask you about that," Beau butted in. "What kinda name is Ahvi? With a name like that, the brother can't be black."

"Ahvi is French and Albanian, but was born and raised in the UK." It made me smile just thinking about my fiancé. I missed my love already and if it weren't for the time difference I probably would have been on the phone right now instead of talking to these two fools.

"Jesus, take the wheel. She done fell in love with a white man." Beau threw his hands in the air and pretended like the rapture was coming.

"First of all, keep your hands on the wheel." I put on my stern voice like my mama so Beau understood I was serious. "And, second, I'm not marrying for race. I'm marrying for love."

"If you're so in love, why is this the first time we're meeting him?" Henry gave me the "I'm on to you" look.

If Henry thought he was going to call my bluff, he had another thing coming. He could throw out all the ridiculous questions he wanted to. *He can never get the best of me.* "Because our lives are busy and I didn't want my fiancé to be exposed to the coonery that is my family."

"Damn, shawty. Why we gotta be coons though?" Beau said, trying to sound as if his feelings weren't hurt.

"Beau, you just called me shawty. Cased closed." We all chuckled out loud. I had to admit there was a piece of me that was a little happy to be in a familiar element. I still wasn't too excited about this whole wedding reunion debacle, but this ride wasn't so bad.

I finally settled back into my seat and took in the scenery. Everything looked so new and different; even just being on the right side of the road felt odd. I could feel Henry's eyes on me and I knew he was plotting his next move. Our silence was broken by this obnoxious ring from his cell phone.

"Wow, can that ring get any louder?" I said, halfway annoyed, halfway joking.

"Uh-oh, that sounds like trouble, bruh," Beau said, peering through the rearview mirror.

Henry rushed to get his phone out of his pocket, looked at it, then quickly put it on silence. I noticed there was only a number that popped up without a name.

"Still popular I see," I said, looking back out the window.

"I'm sure it was probably business," he lied.

"So why didn't you answer it?" *My turn to start calling bluffs.*

"Trick question, bruh," Beau interjected.

I could see the wheels turning in Henry's head as his phone rang again. I burst out into laughter this time. This was exactly why I was happy with my life the way it was. Henry trying to bring his weak game all while other women were calling him was simply hilarious. This wasn't high school, and I was never that easy.

"Why don't we all agree to stay quiet the rest of the ride," I proclaimed. I was not in the mood to be bothered with this foolishness, and I knew how to shut all that down with a quickness. With that being said, Beau turned up the radio and I closed my eyes to dream about being at home with Ahvi.

Chapter 5

Janette

After hearing Henry's answering machine for the fifth time, I slammed the phone down in anger. I didn't know what was happening but I was not a happy camper. I made plans for us to go out to breakfast and I hadn't heard from him all morning. I had worked vigorously for six months wooing Henry and we were going to be together. I composed myself enough to finish getting dressed for Morgan's welcome home party. Every bone in my body ached at the thought of this party, but I wouldn't let Morgan get the best of me this time. I was going to put my big girl panties on and keep my composure through this thing. *As soon as she says "I do," she'll hop back on that plane to London and everything will go back to the way it is supposed to be.*

I put the finishing touches on my makeup and checked myself out in the mirror. *This party may be for Morgan, but all eyes will be on Janette. I am not taking the back seat today.* I grabbed my clutch and proceeded to the door. Before I could touch the handle, the phone rang.

"Henry?" I answered after the second ring, out of breath from rushing to pick it up. All I could hear was heavy breathing and sniffles on the other end.

"Hello. Who is this?" I almost started to hang up, thinking it was a prank call, until I heard my mother's voice.

"Janette, you need to come home. Something's happened."

I could tell that my mother was trying to hold back her hysteria. She only called me Janette when it was something serious, and her being in tears made my stomach drop. I hung up the phone without a response and ran out the door like my hair was on fire.

I almost got into at least three accidents trying to get to my parents' house. As soon as I pulled up, I noticed two police cars in the driveway. I felt my heart sink as I put my car in park and rushed to the door.

The scene in my folks' living room was like something out of a movie. My mother was sobbing on the couch with my brother holding her. One police officer was standing by the fireplace, while the other was sitting directly in front of my mother. I stood still at the front door trying to take it all in.

"Are you Janette Maxson?" the officer who is by the fireplace said as he approached me.

I shook my head in confirmation but kept my eyes on my mother. "What happened? And where is my dad?"

"Why don't you have a seat, Ms. Maxson." The officer tried to nudge me near the couch and I yanked my arm away from him.

"I don't want a seat. I want to know what happened. Mama, where is Dad?" My mother began to cry harder, and everyone in the room seemed like they didn't want to speak.

"Your daddy never came home last night," my mother finally spoke, though it was almost a whisper.

"Ma'am, we found your father's car outside of Speedy's bar this morning. Unfortunately he was deceased inside of the vehicle."

The officer continued talking and my whole world went black. It was like nothing existed anymore. *This has to be a nightmare. Any minute I will wake up and call my fa-*

ther and he will be here. I began pinching myself as hard as I could to try to wake myself up, but nothing changed. The tears began to stream down my face as I dropped to the floor. The officer was quick to catch me and place me beside my mother and brother.

"We won't know for sure until we get the toxicology report, but we believe he died of natural causes," officer number two said. "We are so sorry for your loss, but here is my card and you can contact me anytime." He handed the card to my mother and she clutched it as she continued to sob.

The officers paused before they exited through the front door, leaving the three of us on the couch in silence. I was speechless. I just saw my father the other day and he was perfectly fine. There was no way he could be dead. This had to be a mistake.

"Mama, I'm gonna go make you some tea," my brother finally said. JJ wasn't crying but I could tell he was just as hurt as the rest of us. My daddy and he had a wonderful relationship. They did everything together; he was even named after him. My brother was a macho man but I knew this was eating him up inside. He kissed my mother on the cheek and disappeared into the kitchen.

I scooted closer to my mother and laid my head on her shoulder. We sat and cried in silence, neither one of us knowing what to do next. This was the absolute unthinkable situation. My mother stroked my face for a little while, then wiped her tears dry and got up from the couch.

"I guess I should start making calls to the family." She glanced at their wedding picture that was sitting on the mantle and sniffed back a tear.

I sat there alone on the couch surrounded by my thoughts. My daddy and I weren't extremely close but this was causing me so much pain. I lay down in the fetal position and cried until I fell asleep.

Chapter 6

Morgan

As long as I'd been gone, my folks hadn't changed the house one bit. Everything was exactly how I remembered it. My father still had that rusty truck in the driveway, which I knew was driving my mom crazy. I took a deep breath and finally got out of the car. This was it. I was actually home after eight years. Henry led me in the house while Beau got my bag out of the trunk. Butterflies were jumping all in my stomach as I prepared for what I was walking into.

Walking through the house, my mother decorated it so pretty. There were banners, balloons, and streamers everywhere. The aroma of my mama's cooking filled the air and I could hear old-school nineties music playing in the background. I must admit, my mama went all out. Henry and I rounded the corner into the family room and I was expecting to hear a bunch of people yell out, "Surprise."

"Look who I found." Henry pulled me in front of him and I was greeted by solemn faces. There were at least fifteen people, including my parents, sitting around in silence. I was so confused by what was going on. I knew I wasn't so excited to be coming home, but was everyone upset by it? What kind of party was this?

"Hey, y'all. I'm home," I said, still trying to figure out the situation.

My father finally came to hug and kiss me. I scanned the room and realized that most everyone in the room was crying. Something was really wrong.

"Welcome home, baby. We missed you so much."

"But I'm guessing that's not why everyone is crying. Daddy, what's going on?"

My father took a step back and glanced at my mother to see if she was going to answer my question. I had never seen her in such a state of shock before.

"We just got word that Joe died," my father answered.

"Uncle Bug?" Now it was my turn to be in a state of shock. I couldn't believe what I was hearing. I just talked to Uncle Bug the other day and he was so excited to see me. We had always been close. He was actually my favorite uncle. He called me every week when I moved away, he made sure that I had whatever I needed even when I was doing pageants, we even had our own language. He was truly my favorite uncle. There was no way he was dead.

"How?" I barely got out.

"Not sure, but we think it was a heart attack. The police found him in his car."

This was so awful. I rushed over to my mother's side to console her. She and Uncle Bug were the closest in age out of all their siblings and I knew this was tearing her up.

"Hey now, partay." Beau danced in all excited. As soon as he scanned the room he straightened up. "Dang, who died?"

Henry hit him in the back of the head, trying to give him a hint to calm down. It was silent for a few minutes, with the music still playing in the background like a twisted soundtrack to what was going on.

"All right now. I done cooked all this food and my baby is home, so let's go eat. We'll think about Joe after," my mother finally said as she patted my hands.

Beau was the first one to pop up and head to the dining room. "You ain't got to tell me twice."

"I worry about you sometimes, you know that?" I heard Henry say as he followed him. Everyone else slowly began to move and pile into the dining room. My mother and I stayed seated.

"Mama, are you sure about this? I don't need a party." I honestly didn't want to be bothered with anyone in the first place, until it was absolutely necessary, so I had no problem with this being cancelled.

"Nonsense. This is the first time we've seen you in eight years, we're having this party." She finally took a good look at me and kissed me on my cheek. "I'm so happy to see you. How was your flight?" she asked through tears, and I couldn't tell if they were happy or sad ones.

"It was good. I slept through most of it."

"That's good, baby." She looked around like she was trying to locate something. "Aren't you missing someone?"

"Ahvi had to work this week." I was actually relieved to say those words. I would have hated for this situation to be the first time Ahvi met my family.

"We can't have a wedding without a groom."

"Trust me, there will be a fiancé here for the wedding." I hugged my mother and held on tight. Not being able to do this for almost a decade really made me never want to let her go.

"C'mon, let's go get some food before Beau eats it all." My mother grabbed me and pulled me to the dining room. If I was going to be in Georgia, I sure was going to eat like I was in Georgia.

Over several hours, people came and went to and from my parents' house, giving both their congratulations and their condolences. I got to see cousins and aunts and uncles who I hadn't talked to in a long time. Everybody inquired about Ahvi, and I tried to give them as minimal an amount of information as possible. It was nice to see everyone but nerve-wracking at the same time.

Beau and Henry were the final two to leave the house and I was so happy to finally get settled in. My parents kept my bedroom exactly the same. It was almost surreal to see all the stuff I did throughout my childhood. All of my crowns, sashes, and trophies still lined the walls. Pictures of me when I was little still hung on my mirrors. My mom even kept my favorite teddy bear on the bed. It was like I had stepped into a time machine.

"You happy to be home?" my father asked at the door.

"I think I'm still processing it. It's been a long time." I grabbed my teddy and hopped on my bed. My dad had a smile on his face as he came and sat beside me.

"You know, it's unfair to a father to have his only child move halfway around the world and never come visit him." My father had a tone like he was joking, but I could tell that he was kind of hurt about it.

"I know, Daddy, and I apologize."

He kissed me on my forehead and I knew that everything was all right.

"So Henry seems to be putting his final bid in. You know he's really been successful with that car service business."

Why is Henry even a subject right now? He is not even close to the top of the list of important topics to talk about. I would at least have thought my own daddy would be on my side. "Henry just wants what he can't have. He's always been that way. Besides, you all dragged me thousands of miles to get married here; I'm marrying Ahvi."

My father chuckled, trying to find the words to say. We sat in silence for a few minutes, both of us unsure what our next move was. The sadness hit once again as I remembered that a tragedy just happened.

"Dad," I finally asked, "what are we gonna do about Uncle Bug?"

My father stopped grinning as the memory of Bug's death came flooding back to him. The men in our family were very tough, but a death like this was hard to swallow.

"The only thing we can do. Celebrate his life and keep on moving."

My father stared at the ground for a few minutes without moving. I could tell he was thinking about all the times he and Uncle Bug shared together. They had grown up down the road from each other so they were more than brothers-in-law; they were close friends. He finally jumped out of his daze and kissed me on the forehead.

"Night, baby girl. Get you some rest. I'm sure your mama has plenty for y'all to do tomorrow."

"Night, Daddy."

He closed the door and I walked around my room one more time. I stopped at my vanity mirror, gazing at the grown woman in the reflection. I never thought I would be back here like this: rushed wedding, dead uncle, crazy family reunion. *Lord, I don't know what you're doing up there, but it isn't funny anymore.*

Chapter 7

Henry

I had seven missed calls, four inquiring text messages, and two very angry voice mail messages all from Janette. I knew she would be pissed about me ignoring her phone calls when I was in the car with Morgan, but I wasn't about to take that chance of creating an awkward situation. Besides, I had expected to see her at the party. It was such a tragedy about her father. Junebug was a good dude. He was funny, always had some kind of backwoods wisdom, loved his family, and had a special relationship with Morgan. When Morgan and I finally announced that we were an item the summer before our tenth grade year, he was the one who took me aside and threatened my life if I ever hurt her, or got her pregnant. I thought the main point was "don't get her pregnant." I was more scared of him than I was her own father.

I cleared out my phone and dialed Janette's number. It went straight to voice mail and I hung up before leaving a message. I'd known Janette a long time and I considered her a good friend, but she had been coming on a little strong lately. Dropping by my office to bring me lunch, cooking me dinner at her house, supposedly accidentally bumping into me at places she knew I visited regularly, like the gym, were all becoming a bit much for me. Granted, I accepted the food and the gifts, but, I mean, who would turn down free food?

I tossed the phone on the other side of my bed and lay back down. The beauty of owning your own company was being able to go in whenever you wanted, and this morning I felt like sleeping in. I wanted to reminisce about seeing Morgan. It was the same feeling I had when I saw her in my homeroom in the ninth grade. Growing up with her cousin, we had always been around each other, but it seemed like after puberty hit she started looking a whole lot different to me. Seeing her yesterday, after all this time, made me fall for her all over again. She still had the silkiest bronze skin with those gorgeous hazel eyes; her hair was long and curly, how I'd always liked it, and she still looked like she was the perfect size six. She was even more beautiful than I remembered. She literally took my breath away. I didn't even get to say what I wanted to say to her between that awkward car ride and that depressing welcome home party. I wished I had played it better, especially since her fiancé didn't even come with her.

Every time I tried to get closer to her yesterday, different family members would surround her trying to pry into information about her upcoming nuptials. I overheard her trying to be vague about everything, which was typical Morgan. She never liked people in her business, especially in a town that would spread it like wildfire, but to be a woman about to get married she sure didn't show the signs. She wasn't bragging about how wonderful her soon-to-be husband was, or giving details on where they met, or even how he proposed. I would think if she was so in love, she would at least want to give people a little of her fairytale. I really didn't think she was completely sure about marrying this dude, and I was going to at least try to see if we still had something. If nothing else, I was happy to have her back home.

I stayed in the bed a few more minutes, gazing at the ceiling, before I got up and headed to the shower. Being able to sleep in was cool, but it wasn't in my nature. I needed to get out and be productive. I was still waiting to hear a decision from Don and his business partners about the investment for the new branch of business. The meeting went well but I was always nervous about how these things could go so I needed something to take my mind off it.

The sweltering heat hit me as soon as I walked outside. I lived here all my life and I still hated Georgia in the summertime. It was like the sun had no respect for the people in the South. I jumped in my car and decided to head about an hour outside of town. With everything going on, I needed to visit my mom. She was the only person I could be completely honest with, and I hoped I could catch her on a good day so she could give me her motherly advice. I desperately needed that at the moment.

When I finally pulled into the parking lot, I hesitated on getting out. I hated medical facilities, especially after I blew out my knee. It was cold, it smelled funny, the food was awful, and everybody treated you like some type of burden. I was completely against my mother being here, but I couldn't take care of her by myself anymore.

I got out of the car and began to walk the dim hallways of the nursing home. When I reached her room, the bed was made and none of her personal belongings were in there the way I had set them up.

I went in and checked the drawers and the closet to check for her clothes, and everything was completely empty. I began to panic. If something had happened to my mother they would have called me. I ran outside into the hallway and bumped into a nurse. The clipboard she was holding dropped to the floor and her paperwork spread across the linoleum.

"I apologize about that." I bent down to gather her things and put them back on her clipboard as neatly as I could.

"Didn't anyone ever teach you not to run in halls?" the what seemed like a five foot two nurse said in all her attitude.

"I'm sorry but I'm looking for my mother, Margaret Lloyd. She's supposed to be in this room." I handed her back her clipboard and she snatched it out my hands.

"Ms. Lloyd was moved to a different room. Go down the hall, make a right, and she is the first door on your left."

"Thank you so much," I said in relief, and began taking off down the hallway.

"Mmhmm. Just stop running in my halls."

I completely ignored the nurse's directions, especially after she demanded so nicely, and trotted to my mother's room. When I reached her door, she was sitting in a rocking chair, staring out the window. She had a really nice view of the abundant trees and a small man-made lake that lined the backside of the facility. I figured she probably made a huge scene about having a view until they gave in and switched her room. My mother had always been an outdoors type of girl. She and my grandfather were extremely close and growing up he taught her everything there was to know about fishing, hunting, sports, how to fix things, et cetera.

"Ma." I walked in slowly and squatted down beside her.

"There's my baby boy." She put on a huge grin and grabbed my face to kiss me on my cheek. I grabbed her right hand while it was still holding my face, and kissed the inside of it.

"How you doing today, beautiful?"

"I'm fine. Sittin' here watching the ducks in the water." She folded her hands in her lap and slightly began to rock in her chair. I pulled up a folded chair that was in the corner of the room and sat next to her.

"I see they changed your room."

"Now I told them if I was going to stay here I needed a view. These nurses don't know what the hell they're doing. You know I tried to get them to turn on your game on Saturday and they act like I was speaking Chinese."

I dropped my head and tried to choke back tears. By that statement alone, she wasn't having the best of days.

"Ma, I don't play football anymore. Remember I blew out my knee a few years ago." I hated having to say that every time she had an episode. I didn't want to upset her and I didn't want to have to relive it.

"You remember that game against Madison? You had over two hundred receiving yards and scored four touchdowns."

"Yes, ma'am, I do." I smiled at the memory of one of the best games I had in my high school career. It was the game when four recruiters got to witness in person the magic that was my skills, and the night I knew I was going to play for somebody's Division-I school.

"That was your night, baby. Best wide receiver in Georgia. I'm telling you, Coach should let you run more outside options. No corner can hold you on the outside."

I couldn't help but smile at the fact that my mother could recall my glory days so well. She was always my biggest supporter and my dream of going pro was partly for her, too. When my dad left, I felt it was my job to take care of her the way she deserved to be taken care of. I wanted to give her the big house and nice cars and not have her working two jobs to support me and my brother. I decided not to burst her bubble anymore and just play along.

"I'll make sure to tell him at practice." She patted me on my back and continued to gaze outside the window and rock back and forth.

We sat there in silence for a few minutes as I contemplated what to say next. My mother's dementia was delicate on days like this and I didn't want to get her upset, nor did I feel like I was going to get any advice about the Morgan situation. I never imagined that my mother would be fifty-two in a nursing home with dementia. Both of my grandparents died of Alzheimer's disease, and I knew it was possible for her to have it, but I never knew it would hit her so soon. All I wanted to do was bust her out of here and take her home.

"Ma, I promise you as soon as I'm able I will come and get you out of here," I finally said as I grabbed her hand and kissed it.

"I know, baby. You don't worry about your mama. You just concentrate on going pro."

A single tear rolled down my face and I quickly wiped the back of my hand across my face.

"Yes, ma'am," were the only words I could whisper out of my mouth. I tried to pull myself together before a river of tears flowed. At this very moment I didn't want to think about the Morgan situation, I didn't want to think about the business venture; I just wanted to make my mama happy. She gave up so much for me and I hated that she ended up in this place. I finally gained enough composure to look her in the eyes.

"You know what we need? A Dairy Queen run."

A smile beamed across my mother's face as she got up to go find her purse. It wasn't much, but it was what I could do at the moment to keep her spirits up and get her out of this old people's prison for a while. This was something we did all the time growing up when my mother wanted to treat my brother and me for doing something good. It was fun to laugh and eat ice cream with her. I wanted that feeling again. I needed it right now and I could tell she needed it too.

"Let's go get you some chicken strips and an ice cream sundae."

I put her arm inside of mine and guided her out of her room. Whatever Morgan issues I wanted to talk to my mom about I could deal with on my own. It was better to concentrate on the woman who loved me most anyway.

Chapter 8

Janette

The news of my father's death still stung. My brother and I stayed at my parents' house to try to keep my mother company. Honestly I didn't know how much company I was because all I did was cry all night. I lay in my old bed with the shades drawn so no light could get in. I didn't think I'd ever felt pain like this in my life. *Open-heart surgery with no anesthesia would probably be less painful than this.* I held tight on to my pillow as more tears began to flow. A knock at my door made me suck in hard, trying to compose myself.

"Nettie, you okay?" My brother poked his head around the door, looking to see if I was still alive.

"No, but you can come in." I cut the bedside lamp on and moved over to make room for JJ. He slowly made his way to the bed and put his arms around me. It'd been a long time since my brother had to comfort me like this. JJ and I were five years apart but he had always made sure that he looked out for me. Even when I didn't feel completely loved by my father, I knew I was always my brother's baby.

"How's Mom?" I said through the remainder of my tears.

"Heartbroken, but trying to be strong." He squeezed me tighter to let me know that I didn't have to be strong around him.

"How are you?" I asked him, making sure he wasn't trying to swallow down his pain.

"I'm hoping remembering the good times will make it less painful. Like remember when he tried to teach us how to swim?"

I giggled at the thought of eight-year-old JJ and three-year-old me at the community pool with my dad. "Yeah, and you were so scared to go in the deep end."

JJ began to chuckle with me. "You doggone right I was scared. That was ten feet."

"Daddy didn't think it was so deep because he sure forced you in."

"I can hear his voice now. 'Joe Jr., stop all that hollerin' and kick yo' feet, boy.'"

My brother and I both fell out laughing at his impression of our father. It was so exact to his angry voice; it was almost like Dad was in the room.

"What about the time he almost got to fighting with Mr. Johnson next door about using our trash cans," I said, continuing to laugh hysterically.

"Man, I've never seen two middle-aged men 'bout to put hands on each other over trash cans." The memory of my father out in the yard in his pajamas, dancing around with his fist up like he was in a boxing ring was too much for me to handle. My laughter became uncontrollable and my stomach began to hurt.

"Honestly, though, if Mama hadn't broken it up, I really think Mr. Johnson would've given Daddy a run for his money," JJ continued as he began to control his laughter.

After a few more minutes of the giggles, I finally was able to get myself together. I took deep breaths to calm myself so that I could talk again. "I never realized we really did have some good times with Daddy." I was almost back to a normal voice, with only small traces of giggles.

"Yeah, we really did."

For some reason, JJ's confirmation brought us back down off of our reminiscing high. I didn't think I could actually produce any more tears at this point, but I was becoming depressed all over again. No matter how many funny stories we could tell about Dad, the fact still remained that he wasn't here anymore, and he was never coming back.

"What are we gonna do, Nettie?" This was the first time JJ had no idea what to do next. My father had always taught him to have a game plan and be one step ahead, but I could really hear in his voice that he was lost.

We lay in silence for a few minutes as my wheels began to turn. All of the memories, all of the stories, needed to be shared among family. My father was a big part of the Maxson family equation and he should be respected as such.

"JJ, we need to have Daddy's funeral next weekend." I said it as if it had to be done. I could tell my brother needed time to process.

"Next weekend, as in the family reunion?"

"Why not? Everyone will already be here."

"Yeah, but it's so much going on as we speak. The reunion is jam-packed, then you have Morgan's wedding, and now you want to throw a funeral on top of that?"

I sat up at the mention of Morgan's name and faced my brother. I could feel my blood boiling by the second. This was no longer about her.

"Are you telling me Morgan's little wedding is more important than our father's burial?" I gave my brother that look when I wanted him to say the right thing.

"No, but—"

"But nothing." I cut him off before he could get his thought out. "Daddy was an important part of this family— a family who is planning to celebrate the fact that we are family, next weekend. Why wouldn't Daddy's death be included in that?" I saw my brother contemplating the idea. I could tell he was trying to figure out if there was a more logical solution. We sat in silence for a few minutes as he continued to think.

"You're right," he finally said. "He should be celebrated during the family reunion."

I was so happy my brother was on board. I jumped up and began rummaging through my drawers.

"What are you doing?"

"Looking for clothes. We're going to Beanie's house to tell her." Though my red dress I had put on for the party was fierce, I wasn't going out the house in something I had cried and slept in all night.

I could feel my brother wanting to object to my request, but he held it in. He got up from the bed and left me in the room to get dressed. For some reason I was mildly excited. The death of my father was tragic and heart-breaking, but the fact that this week would no longer be all about Morgan gave me a little joy. I found some old shorts and a tank top that I could put on and headed to the bathroom to take a shower.

An hour later, JJ and I climbed in his truck and pro-ceeded to our aunt's house. In retrospect, Beanie and Uncle Earl lived in walking distance from my folks' house, but this summer heat was beginning to be too much to bear. As we pulled up, my uncle was pulling out. JJ stopped the truck and rolled the window down to speak.

"I was gonna stop by today and see how y'all were doing," my uncle said as he was still rolling down his window.

"We're making it," JJ answered.

"All right, well, I'm headed to the garage. Morgan and Beanie are stirring around in there."

I rolled my eyes at the mentioned of Morgan's name.

"All right, Uncle Earl." JJ rolled the window back up and continued to the house. Everything began to spin as JJ put the truck in park and got out. I couldn't move one muscle of my body to make my way into the house.

"C'mon now, this was your idea." JJ came around to the passenger side and opened my door. I slowly took my seat belt off and took a deep breath. Why was I so nervous all of a sudden? This was something I wanted. I was going to go in this house and demand that my father have the respect that he deserved. I finally got out of the truck.

Inside the house were traces of the party that we missed yesterday. There was a welcome home banner hanging in the foyer, streamers that lined the walls, and a few low-floating balloons. It kind of pissed me off that they were celebrating the return of someone who abandoned her family while my family was in agony. Now I was really motivated to complete this mission. JJ's nose led him into the kitchen where my aunt was cooking breakfast.

"Aunt Beanie." JJ tried his best not to startle her, but she still jumped back at the sound of his deep voice. When she turned around and realized it was us, her face immediately turned somber. She grabbed each one of us without saying a word and hugged us for at least three minutes each. When she released me from her embrace, she quickly turned back to her stove to flip over the sausage patties that were sizzling. I could see her wiping her tears, trying not to show us she was crying.

"Y'all hungry?" were the only words she seemed to be able to get out without bursting into complete tears.

"I don't think either one of us has much of an appetite right now," JJ answered for the both of us. I took a seat at the table and JJ followed suit. We watched her in silence go back and forth, taking food out of the oven and off the stove.

"How's Jean? I'll send food back with y'all if you want it." She never took her eyes off the stove.

"She's seen better days, but she'll get through it." My brother continued to answer. "Aunt Beanie, we came here to talk."

She paused for a moment, then turned around and sat down at the table. My brother looked at me like he was presenting the floor for me to speak. Before I could open my mouth, there she was: the five foot five prodigal daughter in all her former beauty queen glory. Her hair was still just as long and flowing as I remembered, her bronze skin had a glow to it, and even in her pajamas she still looked like a movie star. It pissed me off.

"JJ, Nettie, I didn't know you guys were here. I'm so sorry about Uncle Bug."

JJ got up to hug her and welcome her back home. I stayed right in my seat. I was not here for her. She sat at the table between JJ and Beanie and kissed her mother good morning.

"I know it's early, but have you guys thought about when you want the funeral?" Morgan asked like she was the one who was going to be putting it together.

"That's what we came over to talk about."

"We want to have Daddy's funeral next weekend," I finally said, not giving JJ a chance to finish. Both Morgan and Beanie looked at me like I had seven heads and fourteen tongues spinning in circles.

"Don't you think that's a little soon to plan a funeral?" Beanie asked with a look of confusion spread across her face.

"I figured since everyone will already be here, it would be easier." I glared at Morgan, waiting for her to say something that involved her. Since no one spoke I continued.

"It's important that Daddy is given a proper burial while the family is together."

"Aunt Beanie, we'll take care of all Daddy's arrangements. We just need you to make room in the schedule." JJ tried to make light of things. I personally wouldn't have cared if everything on the schedule got cancelled. We were going to have my Daddy's funeral.

"Fine. I can do that for Junebug," Aunt Beanie finally agreed.

JJ and I both had grins of accomplishment on our faces. We stood up from the table and made our way back to the truck. It might not have been much, but I was satisfied that I got what I wanted. *Now the family can focus on the most important thing—my father. No more of just the Morgan Show.*

Chapter 9

Morgan

Let's go over recent events, shall we? In the last week the normal family reunion went from that to my wedding, now to a funeral. I'm starting to believe that God is Ashton Kutcher because I must be getting punk'd. What type of emotional rollercoaster will we be getting on this weekend? First people will be happy, then sad, then happy again. I was getting motion sickness just thinking about it.

Janette thought she was so convincing with that line, "It's important for everyone to be here for a proper burial." Please, she probably just wanted the attention to be on her instead of anybody else. Ever since we were little kids she had always had a little attitude toward me. Being only a year apart, I could sense there was some competition and rivalry there. I didn't know why she was so hostile. I would have gladly switched roles with her if she wanted it; maybe growing up would have actually been enjoyable.

Now I was stuck with high expectations being placed on me wherever I went in this town, especially now that I'd been dragged into this mess of a wedding. Today my mother had a mother-of-the-bride glow about her. She had everything planned out: wedding dress shopping, then cake tasting, then to the flower shop to pick out a bouquet. I was surprised that she was so into this, especially since only a few hours ago we just added a funeral to the agenda.

"All right, here she is."

I walked out of the dressing room behind Clara, the owner of the bridal boutique. I stepped on the pedestal in one of several dresses that had already been pulled for me.

"Oh my God," my mother gushed, "you look so beautiful."

"I have a feeling you are going to say that about every dress." This was a familiar routine with my mother. Every time I had to try on pageant gowns, she would cry and say how beautiful I was no matter what the dress looked like.

I spun around to get a good look at myself in the full-length mirror. As I examined myself, I had to admit I did look good in the one-shoulder chiffon floor-length dress. It was classic and simple, just how I liked things. I started thinking about what Ahvi's face would look like when I walked down the aisle. I felt like this could be the one. I couldn't believe I was actually enjoying this process.

"Wow, you look breathtaking."

I swiveled around to see Henry standing at the door holding a couple of boxes. This was day two of his amazing reappearing act. The airport and surprise party were one thing, but while I was dress shopping for my wedding? How sick was this man?

"I'm pretty sure stalking is illegal in Georgia." I turned back around to the mirror and continued to gaze at myself. I wasn't going to let Henry's presence distract me.

"Bring the ego down, bridezilla. I'm not here for you. I'm here on business."

I didn't know why, but that comment really stung. Not that I wanted him to be there for me, but he didn't have to be so mean about it. Clara came out with a veil and accessories to jack me up so I could get the full effect.

"Henry owns all of the limousine and car services in Macon," she said as she put a jeweled bracelet on me.

"And I just came to restock Ms. Clara on business cards and flyers." He walked over and put the boxes on the counter, then came and stood right beside me. I stood as still as a statue looking at our reflection staring back at me. For whatever reason, my brain was trying to figure out what would life have been like if we had gone through with the plan we made our senior year.

"We always did look good together," he said, looking at the same reflection I was.

The shop got awkwardly quiet and I could feel every eye in the building, including my mama's, on us. I walked off the pedestal and stomped to the dressing room. It seemed to be the only thing I could do to get everyone to stop gawking at me. What was happening? Between everything that was going on with my family, and what-ever game Henry was trying to play, I felt like I was on a Tilt-A-Whirl and I wanted to get off.

"Honey, are you okay?" I heard my mother's voice through the curtain.

I took a breath before I answered. "Yes, ma'am. Tell Ms. Clara I'll take this one." Without her answering, I heard her walk away from the curtain back into the main area of the shop.

I quickly got out of the dress and threw my regular clothes back on. This thing with Henry was ridiculous and I wasn't going to have it continue for the rest of the week. I hung the dress back on the hanger with the veil and accessories. I came back out into the main area and scanned the room for Henry. I spotted him through the window getting into his car. I dropped the dress on the counter and bolted for the door.

"Ma, you can get any cake you want. I'll meet you at the flower shop."

"But . . ." was the last thing I heard my mother say before I was out of the store.

Henry was about to pull off when I jumped in front of his car. I banged my palm on his hood as hard as I could to get his attention.

"Hey, you got something to say to me, let's talk," I yelled to make sure he could hear me through the glass. I could see out the corner of my eye that people were slowing their walk down to see what the commotion was about.

"Are you crazy? This is a company car," he yelled back as he hopped out of the driver's side.

"Oh, big deal, you own the company." We were face to face in the middle of the street. If there was one thing Henry knew about me, it was that I would never back down from him in an argument. He may have won, but he would always remember he was in a fight with me.

"What's your problem, Morgan?"

"What's your problem? I haven't even been home two days and already you've gotten under my skin. You pop up for no reason saying slick comments to me, for what? Say what you have to say, Henry."

He pulled me by my arm out of the street toward his passenger side. I tried to wiggle my arm from his grasp but the more I moved, the tighter he held on.

"Get in the car." He opened the door and gestured for me to get in.

"Why?" I finally snatched away from him and folded my arms, giving as much black girl attitude as I could muster up. That was something he was used to from high school.

"You wanna talk, we'll talk, but not out here in front of everyone. Get in the car."

I stood there for a moment contemplating if I really wanted to have a conversation with him. Now that I made this dramatic scene, which I was sure would be the talk of the town for the next two days, I didn't know if I actually wanted to hear anything Henry had to say.

"You done made this big scene out here. You might as well go through with it," he said as if he could read my mind.

I finally got in the car and Henry slammed the door. As he got in on his side, I opened my mouth to start firing questions at him. He put his hand up in front of my face to shut down anything I was about to say.

"Not here."

For twenty minutes we drove in silence with old-school Marvin Gaye playing on the radio. I tried to sing along to the words inside my head to keep my mind from racing. I had no idea what Henry was going to say to me and I was a little nervous that I had opened Pandora's box. We pulled up to a creek that had the memories rushing back to my mind.

"You remember this?" Henry said as he turned off the engine.

I hopped out the car and walked through the field, thinking about all the times Henry and I would come out here together. I stopped right at the creek's edge and gazed out at the water. Henry came and stood next to me and I could feel him reliving the moments we shared.

"You remember the first time I brought you out here?"

I shook my head yes, remembering our ninth grade year.

"You had a picnic setup," I said in response.

"Yeah, and I asked you to be my girlfriend."

I smiled at how corny Henry was back then. He tried to be all smooth and Billy Dee with his approach but he was a nervous wreck. Being eaten alive by mosquitoes and ants wasn't helping his game either. However, I did think that his effort was cute.

"It's when we had that awful first kiss," I said as we both laughed. Neither one of us knew exactly what it meant to be boyfriend and girlfriend at the time, but we knew kissing was involved. He tried to imitate one of those passionate kisses you see on a chick flick but all it ended up being was wet and awkward.

"We've had a lot of firsts right here. Our first kiss, the first time I said I love you, the first time we made love."

"What's your point, Henry?" I was becoming tired of this walk down memory lane.

"My point is that we had plans, Morgan. We were supposed to go to college together, and when I went pro, we were going to get married." Henry's voice was beginning to rise, but I could tell it was more out of hurt than anger.

"Plans change, Henry, you know that."

"Why does it seem like I was never in your plans to begin with?"

I remained silent. I couldn't form the words to answer his question honestly.

"The first chance you got you just up and left. No good-bye, no 'I've changed my mind.' You just left." He continued, "And now you've come back to marry this random person and I'm supposed to be cool with that?"

I could feel my eyes welling up as I tried to choke back tears. I cared for Henry a lot and I hated that I hurt him, but I couldn't be who he wanted me to be.

"Henry, I apologize if I hurt you, but I had to do what was right for me."

Henry took a seat on the ground and put his head between his hands. I had no idea that he had been carrying this around for all these years. I took a seat next to him and put my head on his shoulder.

"You know things really went downhill for me after you left. I blew out my knee sophomore year, which ended my football career. I lost my scholarship. I had to come back home and try to take care of my mama."

I felt horrible for not being there for Henry at his darkest moments. I considered him my best friend growing up and I should have been there when he needed me.

"I'm truly sorry, but things turned around and you're doing great now." I needed to keep this conversation going in a positive direction.

"What is it about this Ahvi cat that makes you so sure?" He gazed deep in my eyes, searching for an answer.

"There are certain things about Ahvi that unfortunately you will never have."

"Like?" He continued to hold his glance.

I felt like he was trying to burn a hole through my soul. It was hard to have this conversation with him. I couldn't give him the answers he wanted to hear. "It's complicated." I had to put an end to this conversation. "Look, what we had will never change, but it's in the past. Can we just agree to move on and still be friends?"

I put my hand out in front of him, hoping he would shake it in agreement. He stared at it for a moment then slowly took my hand in his.

We smiled at each other and Henry wrapped his arm around me and kissed my forehead. I never realized how much hurt I had caused by leaving Georgia, but I was glad Henry and I could sort of get back on track. For now this was good enough for me, and I exhaled as we sat back and looked at the creek in silence. Maybe the Lord was finishing His comedy set.

Chapter 10

Janette

I never understood how difficult burying a person was until now. And when you're trying to do it in a week, it definitely adds to the stress. Apparently my parents never made any arrangements for their untimely deaths so JJ and I were stuck to handle it on our own. My mother was completely skeptical about having Daddy's funeral so soon, but I explained to her that the sooner we laid him to rest, the sooner we could begin to heal. She was on board to help but after falling out in the morgue trying to identify his body, JJ and I agreed to handle everything else.

"You know your daddy and I go way back. We used to play pool together, even hustled some folks," Mr. Wyatt said, rubbing his round belly at his desk.

"Yes, sir. That's why we were hoping you would help us out on such short notice." JJ always put on his smooth country-boy bit when he was trying to pull the sympathy card. He had watched my father do it a thousand times.

"As much as I liked Junebug, I'm not sure if I can get you what you want in such a rush."

As good as my brother was, I knew we weren't going to get anywhere if he continued to handle this. Mr. Wyatt owned several businesses in town but his funeral home was the most profitable. Between the teenagers killing each other and the old folks dying of natural causes,

Mr. Wyatt stayed busy. He also had no shame hitting on widows who came to bury their husbands, especially the ones who didn't have enough money to do it properly. If we were going to get what we wanted I had to step up.

"JJ, why don't you give Mr. Wyatt and me a minute alone?" The way Mr. Wyatt perked up in his chair, I could tell he was willing to negotiate. JJ looked very uncomfortable and leaned in toward me.

"Are you sure?" he whispered in my ear.

"Trust me. I'll handle this."

He reluctantly got up and left the office. I stared at Mr. Wyatt for a moment, trying to cleverly calculate my approach. I finally got up from my chair and sashayed around his desk. I stood beside him for a moment, giving him a chance to take in my five foot four thick frame. The fact that I had a slender waist with big hips and thighs was always a plus in the South. I sat on top of his desk in front of him, making sure I hiked my skirt up enough to expose my legs.

"Mr. Wyatt." I began stroking his face. "You can't imagine the heartache my family has gone through in the last couple of days."

"I . . . I think I may have an idea," he stuttered while his eyes gazed up and down my body.

"Then surely you can understand how important this is to us." I continued stroking his face and wiping the little beads of sweat that were beginning to form. "My daddy was a good man and you and I both know he deserves a proper burial."

I took his hand and slowly rubbed it across my thigh. He quivered and exhaled and I tried to contain my laughter. I'd seduced many men but never one of my daddy's friends, and never for something so extreme.

"You're asking for a lot in such a small amount of time and money. I am trying to run a business." He was trying to gain his composure.

I slid off his desk and pressed my face against his cheek. I wrapped his arm around my waist and heard him let out a sigh.

"I know, but we would be so grateful," I whispered in my most seductive voice. I kissed him softly on the lips and I was positive I could feel his pulse. "I promise to repay you."

"I'll see what I can do," he said with his eyes still closed.

"Great." I had put my regular voice back on and straightened out my skirt. "I'll expect a viewing of the body, transportation, and a burial plot next to my granddaddy. Oh, and don't be cheap with the casket. You do still owe my father twenty-five hundred dollars." I flashed a grin at him and walked out the office, leaving him speechless in his chair to contemplate what just happened.

"What happened? Is he going to do it?" JJ jumped out of the chair he was sitting in in the waiting area.

"Don't worry, everything is handled."

"What did you do?" His tone insinuated that he didn't trust my methods of negotiation with Mr. Wyatt. As much as I would have loved to reassure him that I was on my best behavior, I just gave him a smirk and proceeded to his truck.

As soon as I jumped in and shut the door behind me, I immediately pulled my phone out of my purse and turned it back on. Every time I had to turn my phone off a piece of me died for fear that I was missing out on something important. I was hoping to see a missed call or text from Henry since I hadn't heard from him all day. Once my screen lit up, a voice mail from Millie flashed. If Millie left a message it either had something to do with the shop or some juicy gossip.

"Girl, you would not believe what I saw today. It's too juicy to leave on a message. Call me back, honey."

Millie's voice blared through my phone. See what I mean? I always missed something. I knew this had to be good. Whenever she left a message to tell me that she couldn't tell me something through a message, it was deep. I hung up my voice mail and before I could even dial the number back, Millie's name popped up on my screen.

"I was just getting ready to call you back," I answered.

"Chile, you was takin' too long." Another sign Millie had some real good dirt; she talked like she'd been working in the field for twenty years.

"Well, excuse me for trying to handle my daddy's death."

"Well, honey, you 'bout to die when you hear what I'm finna tell you. So I was at the nail shop 'cause you know how my baby Ray loves for me to keep my stuff tight," she began.

"Hold up. If you were getting your nails done, who was at the boutique?" I loved hearing gossip but I loved my money more. If this story led to "and somebody broke in," I wasn't going to be the one who was gonna die.

"Keta and Treece, but that's beside the point. I was at the nail shop minding my own business when all of a sudden I hear a female yellin' out in the street. Now you know I'm thinking it's Walt's crazy baby mama Tiffany just finding out he got that girl Destiny pregnant who works down at that new topless bar."

Millie was in rare form. It had been awhile since I heard a story where she was trying to be suspenseful. Background stories and sliding other people's business into the main feature always meant that the story was a good one.

"So I told Ming Ye to stop working on my nails and rushed to the window to see her go off on him while he was at work. Girl, you wouldn't believe who I saw with my own two eyes arguing in the middle of the street."

I knew this was my cue to interject. "Who?" I asked like an excited five-year-old during story time.

"Henry and Morgan."

It was like the world stopped turning. My whole body tensed up, my stomach dropped, and my heart began to beat faster. *I know she didn't just say Henry . . . my Henry.*

"Henry who?" Maybe it was another Henry. Maybe I was hearing things.

"Henry Lloyd. You know tall, muscular, milk chocolate, pretty smile. The Henry you been pining over for two years and all over for the last six months. That Henry. Girl, they were all in the streets making a big ol' scene. Then they got in his car and left."

Millie was telling this story like it was no big deal. Like this wasn't catastrophic to my life. I worked hard to get that boy's attention and I'd be damned if her royal highness was gonna stroll her happy self up in my town and take my man. This was not going down.

"Millie, get to the store."

"But, Ray and I—"

I hung up the phone before she could even finish her sentence. I didn't have time to deal with issues with the boutique as well as this situation.

"Everything okay?" JJ finally spoke. For a minute, I completely forgot he was even there.

"Just drop me at my car. I have some business to handle."

I could feel every ounce of blood in my body boiling. *Who does Morgan think she is?* Her main objective for coming back home was to get married, not to try to ruin my life for a second time. I was going to get to the bottom of this today.

Chapter 11

Henry

I continued to play the scene between me and Morgan over and over in my head as I drove her back to town to catch up with her mother. The silence between us in the car seemed to be extremely loud and was quite awkward. I could tell she was uncomfortable too because I caught her shifting in her seat out of the corner of my eye. I wanted to say something but I felt like silence was the best thing we needed right now. Maybe she was right. Maybe I was holding on to something that I needed to let go. She had moved on, maybe I should have too.

Regardless of the fact, it was still hard to watch my first love—hell, my only love—get married to someone else. I pulled up to the flower shop and parked my car next to Mrs. Willis's. I cut off the engine and we sat in silence a few minutes longer. I tapped my thumbs on the bottom of my steering wheel, waiting for her to either get out or say something.

"Look, Henry," she finally said, "I hope we can move past this."

"Yeah, sure," I replied in a monotone voice. I still had no idea what to make of the situation.

"I mean, I don't want it to be weird between us."

"Weird? Why would it be weird?" I had a feeling even though we had our little pep talk, things were still going to be awkward between us. At this point though, I didn't want to look like any more of a punk.

"So you're still coming to the wedding?" I couldn't tell if her question was her way of inviting me or hoping I would say no because she told me to move on.

"How else are you going to get limo service?"

She gave me a slight smirk, took off her seat belt, and leaned across to kiss me on the cheek. It sent mixed emotions through my body. It was good to feel her genuine warmth around me again, but the cheek kiss felt like I had gotten second place and that was the best consolation prize I could get. She got out of the car and went inside the shop. I sat and watched her for a moment through the glass in front of the shop before I decided to finally head home. This whole situation wasn't turning out in my favor and I just wanted to go home, take a shower, and regroup.

Walking into my house, I spotted Beau on my couch, holding a beer, with a half-eaten sandwich on my coffee table and watching ESPN. It was typical of him to just drop by and let himself in even when I wasn't home.

"Why are you not at work where I pay you to be instead of in my house eating my food and watching my cable?" I grabbed the remote off the table and turned the TV off.

"I just finished my last pickup 'bout an hour ago and I came over to see what my best friend was doing. Plus I was hungry." He bent over to pick up his sandwich and took a bite.

"I bet you were." I dropped my keys on the mantle and walked in the kitchen to grab a beer. I was hot, I was irritated, and alcohol appeared to be the only one that understood me right now.

"So what happened?" Beau yelled from the couch with a mouthful of food.

I walked back into the living room and flopped down beside him. "What happened with what?"

"With you and Morgan. Everybody is talking about how you two had a big fight in front of Clara's where she slapped you and called you a jealous bastard and then you threw her in the car and drove off."

This was completely typical of this town. This only happened a few hours ago and now it was spreading like wildfire. With the wrong information, I might add. I shook my head and took a swig of my beer before answering him.

"So did you do it?" he continued.

"Do what, Beau?"

"You know, have that good ol' angry 'I missed you' sex. That usually be the best sex 'cause of all that built-up aggression."

I swear Beau is such an idiot. I loved him like a brother, but I seriously thought his mama should have held him back a couple of grades to allow his brain to catch up with that big-ass body of his.

"First of all, everybody talking about something and have no clue what they're sayin'. None of that happened. Second, what the hell are you talkin' about? 'I miss you' sex?"

"You know, y'all have a little argument, you bring her back here and give her some act right."

Nothing about what was coming out of Beau's mouth surprised me but it always amazed me that he never felt uncomfortable talking like this about his own cousin.

"We talked, Beau. I took her to the creek and we talked." I took another swig of my beer and sank down in my seat.

"Damn, man. Well, if anybody asks, you might wanna go with my version, 'cause it don't sound like that talk worked out in your favor."

"Get out, Beau." I stood up from the couch and walked back into the kitchen. I didn't want nor have time for this conversation. I'd already been defeated once today; I didn't need a play-by-play recap about it.

"Chill, man, don't be like that." Beau followed me into the kitchen and took a seat at the table. "All jokes aside. What did she say?"

I took a deep breath, another drink of beer, and replayed the discussion from earlier. I tried to figure out what part of it I could tell Beau without looking like a total chump.

"She said she appreciated what we had in the past, but we both moved on."

"That was it?" The look on his face was a mixture of confusion and disappointment.

"That was the gist of it. I agreed and took her back into town." I grabbed another beer out of the refrigerator and tried to chug it in one gulp.

"Not to get in your business or nothing . . ." Beau began.

"Right, because you've been doing such a wonderful job of that already." *Why do people start off with statements like that knowing good and well they are either already in your business or about to be all up in your business?*

"But," he continued, "I don't think you should go out like that."

"Well, enlighten me, Beau. What do you think I should do?" I sounded sarcastic, but I was a little interested in what he had in mind. I was out of a game plan and wouldn't mind a different strategy.

"Fight for your woman, dawg. I know I joke a lot but if you love her, you can't just accept the 'let's just be friends' line."

Beau had a great point, but I honestly wasn't sure if I loved her because of our history together or I was just in my feelings about how she left things. I needed to figure out if I wanted her back or if I just needed some type of closure.

"What did you have in mind?" I was curious to see what Beau could come up with and if it was even worth the risk.

"I don't know, man. Who do I look like, the dude from *Taken?*"

Was this fool serious? This Negro sat here and suggested I do something but didn't have a plan to help me out? *I swear this man is more frustrating than a toddler.*

"No, you look like the idiot who came up with the idea. So either give me something I can work with or shut the hell up and get out."

"All right, man, damn. Just chill."

We sat in silence for a few minutes and I could tell that Beau was really thinking hard. He shifted in his seat a couple times, rubbed his chin, and even scratched his head. It was quite the performance. I didn't think I'd ever seen him think so hard except when he was before a judge.

"All right, I got it." He put his hands up like he had come up with the most brilliant idea.

"Shoot." It couldn't be any worse than telling people Morgan and I had angry "I miss you" sex.

"We should go see what you're up against."

I was wrong. It was worse than the angry "I miss you" sex.

"Let me get this straight. You want us to fly to London to spy on Morgan's fiancé."

"Yeah, I want us to fly to London on the private jet I rented this morning." His sarcasm actually settled my mind. "No, fool," he continued. "I want us to go to the airport whenever she goes to pick him up and see what your competition is. Who knows, he may be some old, fat white cat she's only marrying for money."

That actually wasn't a bad idea. It never hurt to look. Maybe I could determine whether to pursue this any further if I saw her actually moving on with my own eyes.

I had to hand it to Beau, he kind of came through with that one. I was a little upset I didn't think of it first.

"So how do we go about finding out when she's going to get him?"

"Leave that to me, 'cause clearly Morgan is suckin' out all the finesse you ever had."

"Okay, now you can really get out."

We both laughed and I began to feel better about the situation. Maybe I wasn't out of the game just yet. My grandfather used to say, "It doesn't matter how many points you're down, nobody has won until the clock hits zero in the fourth quarter." I didn't think the time clock had run out yet, and I planned to play the entire sixty minutes.

Chapter 12

Morgan

The conversation with Henry was a little intense but I was kind of glad he got it off his chest. Maybe now we could get through this sham of a weekend without any more big dramatic scenes. I had Henry drop me off at the flower shop where my mother was already waiting for me. The look on her face when I walked in was a mixture of shock, embarrassment, and a little entertainment. I didn't think she knew what to make of the situation, and honestly neither did I. *I swear this town takes me out of my element.*

"So what kind of cake did you pick?" I didn't think trying to pretend like nothing happened was going to fly with my mother but it was worth a shot.

"Don't think you can waltz up in here like nothing happened after that scene you made a few hours ago."

I knew it wasn't going to work. I was 96 percent sure that black mamas were mind readers.

"Mama, I apologize for running out and causing a scene earlier, but Henry and I needed to get some things straight in order for everyone to move on."

"Well, I hope y'all got it out of your systems. And your cake is marble with cream cheese icing." My mother had this matter-of-fact type of tone as she began sifting through flowers.

"Mom, we can't have marble cake. Ahvi is allergic to chocolate."

"Well, if the person who would have known better was there maybe she would have had input on the cake. I thought it was sort of symbolic, plus you love marble cake."

I had no argument for my mother. She was the one throwing this all together and I did just leave without warning. Besides, she was right, I really did love marble cake. Maybe I could purchase Ahvi a second cake. I kissed my mom on the cheek as my subtle way of thanking her, and began to look through flowers with her. I had no idea what I was doing. I was never a lover of flowers. I couldn't wrap my mind around the concept indulging in something that died quickly. It all seemed quite pointless to me, but this was the part that I knew Ahvi would really appreciate.

Growing up, Ahvi expressed that flowers were always something special. The colors, the smell, the structure of each individual petal were mere sprinkles of the splendor of God. When we first started dating, Ahvi took me to this beautiful lavender field that was way out in the countryside. It had to be as big as three football fields with rows and rows of purple flowers. It wasn't like anything I had ever seen before. It was so majestic and peaceful. I ran through that field like I was Celie from *The Color Purple*. Ahvi packed us a picnic lunch and we sat between the rows of flowers and ate, laughed, and talked about life and our future plans. It was one of the moments I knew I was falling in love.

"Mom, I want lavender flowers," I said eagerly, coming out of my daydream.

Before my mother could respond to me her phone rang. She fumbled trying to get it out of her purse and answered it as soon as it was in her hands.

"Hello . . . hello," she said, slightly out of breath from the scuffle she just had. All I could hear on the other line was a mumbling of what sounded like a woman's voice. My mother confirmed that she was who the caller wanted and became immediately still when the caller responded. It was as if my mother had seen, or rather heard, a ghost. I tried to ask her what was going on silently but she didn't respond. Instead, she rushed out the shop, dropping the Casablanca lilies she was looking at previously.

I watched her closely through the window as she paced back and forth on the sidewalk. I had never seen my mother like this. She was fidgety and nervous. I could see her explaining herself through her hand gestures. She wiped freshly formed sweat off her forehead but I couldn't tell if that was because of the phone call or because it was twenty degrees past the temperature of hell outside. I wanted to go outside and see what was going on but she hung up the phone and returned inside.

"So you were saying something about lavender." She acted like the last two minutes didn't just occur.

"Uh, who was that on the phone?" I hoped she didn't think I was going to let her off that easy.

"Oh, nobody . . . Just a wrong number." She began rummaging through the flowers again, but I could tell her hands were shaking. Now, my mother was a lot of things, but a liar she was not. *A two-minute phone call for a wrong number? Who does she think she is fooling?*

"That was quite a long conversation for a wrong number."

"Girl, you know how white folks are. They gotta go into this whole explanation on how and why they got your phone number."

I almost took that excuse until I remembered that she acknowledged who she was. My mother was hiding something, and if she couldn't tell me about a phone call, it must have been big. I started to continue my interrogation when my phone rang.

"Hello," I answered reluctantly without even looking at the caller ID.

"Guess what I'm doing right now." The sound of that voice coming through my speaker put a huge smile on my face.

"Standing in our bedroom naked, dripping from the shower you just took." The thought of that image had my body tingling, which was immediately shut down by the look of shock on my mother's face from my comment. I completely forgot she was standing right there. I quickly swiveled my body in the opposite direction and walked away from her before I say any more sexual things to my fiancé.

"Close, I'm packing. In a little less than two days I will once again be in your arms." Ahvi sounded so excited, which made me extremely nervous.

"Babe, are we really sure we want to do this? I mean you could not make your flight and I'll just call the whole thing off."

I had to admit that the wedding planning was giving beautiful flashes of why I loved my fiancé, but hearing Ahvi's voice snapped me back to the reality that we had to deal with my entire family. I started getting cold feet.

"Why would we back out now? You're already there and I think it's past time I meet your family."

I could tell Ahvi wanted me to say something reassuring but I had no response. I honestly didn't know how well this family meeting would go down because they hadn't really been informed on all the details of me and Ahvi. It was complicated and I hadn't found the words to tell my parents everything.

"You haven't told them yet have you?" Ahvi said, reading my thoughts. I guessed my silence was a dead giveaway.

"Babe . . ."

"Oh, Morgan." I could hear the disappointment. "It's all making sense. Your parents have no bloody idea, do they?"

"I'm sorry. And I know I said I would, but I think it's best if we tell them together."

"Well, it doesn't look like we have another choice, do we?"

I hated that I put Ahvi in this position, but for the record I never wanted to do this. I had to smooth things over because as crazy as this wedding/funeral/reunion thing already was, it was going to completely suck if the other half of my team was unhappy with me.

"Please don't be angry with me. With the craziness of this rushed wedding, my uncle dying, and my self-absorbed cousin wanting the funeral the same day, I just haven't gotten a chance." I knew that would pull on Ahvi's heartstrings to get this team back on one accord.

"Wait, your family is having your uncle's funeral on the same day as the wedding and the banquet?"

I had been so busy I completely forgot to tell Ahvi that new piece of information. *Well, I guess now is as good a time as any to understand the dealings of my family.*

"Do you see why I didn't want to come down here in the first place? And I think my mom is hiding something from me."

"Well, maybe it's a surprise for the wedding." I wished I could believe Ahvi's optimism but the way my mother acted didn't seem like it was a wedding secret.

"Getting married here is surprise enough. I'm going to find out what she's hiding." I turned back to see where my mother was in the shop and if she was listening to my conversation. She was enthralled with the white roses so I knew she wasn't paying any attention to me.

"Morgan, let it alone. Your mum is probably doing something special. Don't ruin it. I love you and I'll see you in a couple of days."

"Love you too."

I hung up the phone and returned to the task at hand. My mom had inserted all different types of purple flowers in this beautiful bouquet. She was humming but I could tell in her face that she had something on her mind. I wanted to ask her about it, but I didn't want her to try to tell me any more lies. I knew when my mother was hiding a good surprise and this was not a good surprise. Whatever she was hiding I was going to find out what it was. I was done with surprises in this family.

Chapter 13

Janette

It took me an hour to finally catch up with Henry. His drivers at his office told me that he went and did drop offs around town early this morning and hadn't been back since. I tried to see if he was still out and ended up at his house. I wanted to try to prepare myself with what I wanted to say to him, but the thought of him and Morgan together just made my adrenaline rush. I quickly jumped out of my car and scurried to knock on the door. I walked back and forth on the porch, gathering my thoughts. I had to remind myself not to break out into the jealous baby mama routine.

Henry finally answered the door and every breath I had seemed to leave my body when I saw him. He was dressed in only basketball shorts and socks. His chest and arms were glistening from the beads of water he was still wiping off with a towel. I wasn't sure if he had just taken a shower or finished working out. Either way I was turned on. I tried to straighten out my skirt and hair to make sure I was presentable.

"What are you doing here, Janette?"

I tried to find words but my eyes kept following beads of water down his beautiful six pack. He was absolutely gorgeous and for a second I completely forgot why I was even standing on his porch.

"Janette?" Henry snapped me out of my gaze.

"Um, I wanted to talk to you." He looked at me like he was waiting for me to continue. I started to get heated all over again. We had been involved for several months and all of a sudden Morgan was back in town and he was treating me like some random chick.

"Can I come in?" I tried to hold back my attitude, but I could feel it seeping out. He dropped his head and moved out of the doorway for me to come in.

I walked into the living room and tried to get familiar with the space again. Millie used to always tell me, "Whenever you're going somewhere for a confrontation, always be aware of your surroundings." I had only been to Henry's house once so it was almost like a new space. A picture frame on his side table next to the couch caught my eye. It was a prom picture of him and Morgan from senior year. They looked so young and happy, which made me sick to my stomach. Why did he even still have this picture?

"So what's up?" Henry seemed so nonchalant and it actually hurt my feelings. I cared for him and he was acting like we had nothing going on. I could feel my attitude kick into high gear.

"You tell me." I continued to stand in front of him and folded my arms. This was my "preparing for battle" stance.

"You came over here. So if you have something to say, then say it."

I was so appalled. I had been through a lot these last couple of days and I would at least have thought he would have cared a little.

"You do know my daddy died right?" I was trying to choke back my tears. It was really hard for me to say that out loud.

Henry dropped his head and sighed. "I know and I'm sorry. I tried to call you but your phone was off."

"You couldn't come by to make sure I was okay?" I stared at him with piercing eyes, waiting for him to look up at me.

"Janette, I apologize. Are you here to punish me?"

I finally took a seat next to him. "I'm here to find out what's going on with us." I tried to put my hand on his knee but he jumped back a little bit.

"Wait, what do you mean 'us'? Who is 'us'?" He really seemed surprised at the words that were coming out of my mouth, which was surprising to me.

"You and me, Henry." I went to reach for him again and he jumped off the couch.

"Janette, I'm sorry your dad passed and all but I was not under the impression that there was a you and me." He began pacing the floor and I couldn't believe where this conversation had gone. Was he actually serious right now? All the time and energy I put into this man and he wasn't under the impression that there was an 'us'? Oh, he was about to feel 'us' real quick.

"Henry, what are you talking about? We're involved."

"Whoa, involved is a strong word." He stopped pacing and put his hands on his hips. He looked at me like he was waiting for me to come up with a different description.

"So what would you call it?" I could feel my temperature rising by the second.

"We got drunk one night at the bar and had sex."

There it was. The one button I was waiting for him to push to make me explode. He really just tried to play me. I didn't know who he thought he was talking to but I was Phil Jackson up in this thang. I didn't get played; I coached the players.

"Excuse me?" I got up from the couch and walked toward him slowly. "How dare you open up your mouth to even form that sentence to me."

Henry kept quiet. I could tell in his eyes he was a little nervous about what was about to happen next. Back in the day, I would have never stood toe to toe with someone, but it was a new day and people had to be reminded who I had become.

"Listen," he began cautiously. "I apologize for how harsh the comment came out but it's true. What happened that night was a mistake. I was reminiscing about my life and got caught up in my feelings. You were there and it just happened."

"So why did you start kickin' it with me if it was such a mistake?" I got back into my folded-arm stance. At this point it was the only thing I could do to keep me from hauling off and smacking him.

"Kickin' it? Janette, we've been to lunch like twice and dinner once. I appreciate your friendship but I'm still trying to get over Morgan."

Those words felt like a dagger to my heart. After all these years, Morgan still had a hold on the things that I wanted; always making me feel second rate. *Well, this ain't 2004 and I'm not sixteen anymore.* I was going to get what I deserved.

"So that's what this is about?" I started raising my voice. "The pageant princess skips back into town and all of a sudden I'm not good enough? That's why you're out here making public scenes in the street? What did you do? Take her somewhere and try to rekindle what you two had, huh? Did you sleep with her? Make her think twice about not marrying you?" Each question I posed was louder than the one before it. My whole body was hot and I could feel my knees shaking.

"That ain't none of your damn business." Henry walked right up in my face. I could see the beads of sweat forming on his forehead. "I don't have to explain myself to you."

We stood there face to face, staring at each other angrily. I searched his eyes and I could tell that whatever happened between him and Morgan today didn't work out in his favor. I knew that my words got to him and that gave me slight pleasure. I hit a soft spot for him just like he did me and I knew how to use that to my advantage. I smirked and finally broke eye contact with him.

"Let me clear some things up for you because obviously you are confused." I walked back to the couch and sat down slowly. I crossed my legs and placed my hands on my lap. "I am nobody's one-night stand. What we have going on is something, whether you were clear about it or not. Now I know you have history with Morgan, but that's exactly what it is . . . history. She left and moved on and she's getting married this weekend. If you were her concern, don't you think things would have been different?"

I could see the wheels turning in Henry's head. He battled with trying to be angry and coming to realize what I was saying was true.

"I know it hurts," I continued. "But that's what she does. She only worries about herself. Now do you really want to continue pining over someone who hurt you when you have a perfectly good woman right here who is willing to make you happy?"

I uncrossed my legs and got up from the couch. I walked over to Henry slowly and caressed his arm. He didn't flinch this time. I traced his chest and abs with my other hand and felt him shiver a little from my touch. I wanted to let him know that this wasn't a mistake. He lifted my head up gently and our eyes met each other. I felt a tingle down my spine and my heart began skipping beats. I stood up on my tippy toes and placed a soft, sensual kiss on his lips.

It was like electricity passed through us. I knew he felt it too because he wrapped his arms around my waist and pulled me in closer. I felt his heart beat against my chest and it excited me. I kissed him with all the passion I could muster up. He moved his hands down my body and grabbed my thighs. I held on tight to the back of his neck as he lifted me up around his waist. He walked me back to the couch and laid me down slowly.

All types of emotions began to rush over me. I was so confused about what I was feeling. I was happy to be in this moment but tears began to flow uncontrollably. Henry finally broke our kiss and took a second to look me in my face. His expression was so sweet and it made the tears flow even more. He gave me a short kiss on the lips and then began to kiss my tears away. I knew this was what I deserved and I planned on making sure that it was never ripped away from me.

Chapter 14

Morgan

All night that phone call my mother received would not leave my thoughts. I wanted to confront her several times but we already went down that road, and getting Daddy involved was not an option. This morning I got up on a mission. I was going to find out what my mother was hiding. If it had something to do with the upcoming weekend then there had to be some traces of it in the house somewhere.

Daddy was up and out the house to work at the garage. He was really putting in hard hours to try to get as much money as he could to help out with the wedding expenses. I also thought it was an excuse not to help with any of Mama's planning. He didn't mind providing, but he wasn't trying to pick out nothing.

Mom and I had breakfast in silence while she read the newspaper and I tried to devise a plan. It was unlike her to sit at the breakfast table and not have anything to say, especially with so much going on. There was definitely something up.

"So what are the plans for today?" I finally asked.

"I have to go run some errands for the reunion," she answered without even lifting her eyes from the newspaper. "You want to come?"

"Can I pass? I want to write out my vows before Ahvi gets here."

It was perfect that she had to leave the house, so I could snoop without getting caught. Errands that had to deal with event planning were guaranteed to keep her away for a few hours. She glanced at the clock on the stove and quickly closed her newspaper.

"I better get a move on." She got up and kissed me on the forehead. "You'll clean up the kitchen, baby?"

She didn't even wait for me to say, "Yes, ma'am," before she darted out the kitchen. I listened carefully to make sure she was in the shower before I moved from my seat. Ten minutes passed and I eased out of my chair and lightly ran toward my parents' room. My mother always kept her purse in the same chair by her bed ever since I was a little girl. I wanted to see if anything related to that phone call was going to be leaving the house with her.

I gently pushed the door open and paused to reassure myself that she was still in the shower. When she started the second verse of "Amazing Grace," I knew I was in the clear. I spotted her purse by the chair and crept over to it. I felt so bad going through my mother's things but I had to find out what was going on. If it had something to do with the wedding I'd just leave the surprise for Ahvi.

I sifted through her bag but didn't find anything that looked out of the ordinary. After thoroughly investigating her pocketbook, I put everything back in place and was about to look in the bedside table when the shower water turned off. My body immediately went into panic mode. I bolted out of that room and ran to the kitchen. I scrambled around looking for something to do that didn't look suspicious. I turned on the faucet and began gathering dishes in the sink. My heart was pounding a mile a minute. I hadn't felt a rush like that since I was a kid, sneaking around my parents' room trying to find my Christmas or birthday presents.

I cleaned the kitchen and went to my room to wait her out. A few minutes later I heard her yell good-bye to me and head out the front door. I waited until I heard the engine turn on and her drive away before I bolted back to my parents' room. I proceeded to the drawer I was going to look in before my mama got out of the shower. I rummaged through it with no luck of anything. I slammed the drawer in frustration and a cup that was sitting on top fell to the floor and rolled under the bed.

I lay down on my stomach to retrieve it and noticed a black lockbox. I scooted my body as far as I could under my parents' bed to grab it from the middle of the floor. I struggled to reach it and after a couple minutes of flailing my hand back and forth, I finally took hold of the handle and pulled it from under the bed.

I looked at the box like I had struck gold. I wasn't sure that whatever was in it had anything to do with what my mother was hiding, but I knew I had to get in it. I tried jiggling and prying it open, but realized that there was no way I was getting in that thing without a key. I got up from the floor and looked for something I could pick the lock with. I finally found a bobby pin in the bathroom and rushed back to the floor. I had no idea what I was doing but I figured I'd seen enough action movies where the girls pick steel trapdoors with a chopstick from their hair that I could break into a lockbox. I separated the ends just enough that they fit into the lock at both ends and tried to feel my way around. After about a ten-minute battle with the thing, I heard something click.

"What exactly are you doing?" The deep voice startled me and I jumped and screamed at the same time. I tried to slide the box back under the bed as quickly as I could without being extremely suspicious.

"Seriously?" I finally said after I realized it was Beau. "Don't you know what a doorbell is? You almost gave me a heart attack." I took deep breaths in and out to try to slow my heart rate. I could feel it pounding ridiculously fast against my chest.

"Well, I would've knocked if the door wasn't already open."

I guessed my mother didn't close it all the way when she was rushing out of here, which made me even more certain that something was going on.

"What are you doing in here anyway? You know the first rule in a black home is never go in your folks' bedroom without permission. I don't care how old you are," Beau said as he leaped his big self across my parents' bed.

"If that's the first rule then why are you making yourself so comfortable in here?" I finally got my heart to calm down and got up off the floor.

"This ain't my folks' room."

I had to admit, as dumb as his logic was, he kind of had a point. I scanned over everything to make sure nothing was too noticeably out of place and then walked out the room.

"What are you doing over here anyway? Shouldn't you be working for Henry?" I said as Beau followed me out into the living room.

"Dang, a brotha can't get no love for wanting to come see his favorite cousin, who's been MIA for eight years, on his day off?" Beau should have really reconsidered this whole chauffeuring thing and tried his hand at acting, because he was always extremely dramatic.

"So you came all the way over here just to kick it with me?"

"Of course. I haven't seen you in forever. I was tryin'a get up with you."

"You saw me the other day." I laughed a little after that comment because we both knew I was going there.

"Whatever, cuz. Go throw some clothes on and let's go grab something to drink."

"Beau, it's like ten in the morning." I couldn't imagine any bar being open this early in the day, and if there was, who was that depressed that they needed to drink this early? Then again, this place did tend to drive people to the bottle.

"Then get somethin' with orange juice in it."

I wanted to refuse the invitation and get back to the matter at hand, but Beau was about the most fun cousin I had and I really didn't mind catching up with him. It had been awhile and I missed having him around to joke with. He reminded me a lot of my uncle Bug and that was something I didn't want to pass up. I went and got dressed as quickly as I could to speed this process up.

Drinking before noon didn't seem like such a crazy idea after I had two shots of tequila and a beer in me. Laughing, talking, and drinking with my cousin actually felt like old times. Believe it or not, there were moments growing up that I was quite fond of. I loved the nights when Beau, Henry, a few other of my cousins and I would sneak down to the creek and drink beer by a little bonfire. It helped to not make Georgia a complete hellhole for me.

"Can you believe the type of coonery that's about to go down with this family this weekend?" I slurred a little. I hadn't drunk tequila since college and I could feel it kicking in.

"Did you expect something different?" Beau smirked and took a swallow of his beer.

"No, not really. I just didn't think we could fit it in all in one day." I started laughing extremely hard at my own statement. I couldn't tell if it was the alcohol or just the thought of my family actual playing major event roulette. Whichever one it was, my laughter was becoming uncontrollable.

"I still can't believe you gettin' married," Beau said, not acknowledging me giggling like a hyena.

I took deep breaths to calm myself. I could sense this was about to be a sentimental moment and I wanted to be serious for it. "To be honest with you, Beau, neither can I." I took a sip of beer and looked down at the modest solitaire diamond engagement ring on my left hand.

"Do you love him?"

"Him who?" I responded without looking up from my hand.

"Your fiancé," Beau said with a chuckle that sounded like he was trying to mask confusion.

"Oh, yeah, of course. I just kind of let go of the idea of marriage for a while, that's all."

We sat in silence for a while, sipping on our beers, waiting for the other to make a move. The closer this weekend got, the more apprehensive I became and I wasn't sure how any of it would turn out.

"So are we ever gonna meet the cat or he'll just appear from a puff of smoke at the altar?"

I chuckled at Beau's comment, although it didn't really sound like a bad idea. "Ahvi gets into Atlanta around two tomorrow."

"Well, that's what's up. I know everybody can't wait to meet him."

Without responding, I ordered us another round of shots and beer. Tomorrow the person I planned to spend the rest of my life with would meet the family I tried so desperately to avoid the past couple years. On top of which we had to deal with funerals and family reunion events all at once. I wasn't sure whether I was going to be able to get through any of it, but at this moment I wasn't trying to be sober to think about it.

Chapter 15

Henry

I think it was safe to say that I had officially purchased a one-way ticket straight to hell. I didn't know what I was thinking hooking up with Janette all over again. I knew I wasn't perfect, but I also wasn't the type of guy who tried to get his ex-girlfriend back one minute, then slept with her first cousin the next. If this was anybody else maybe I wouldn't feel so bad, but I think sleeping with family members was an unforgivable offense.

I glanced over at Janette sleeping peacefully with a slight smirk on her face. It was like she had accomplished some big mission and it kind of freaked me out. I tried to slide my arm that she was lying on out from under her so I could go to the bathroom. I needed a game plan on how I was going to fix the situation. I successfully freed most of my arm without waking her, but tried to pull my hand out too quickly and fell hard on the floor.

"Henry, you okay?" Janette popped up out of her sleep.

"Yup, just clumsy, that's all." I hopped up from the floor and put on a pair of basketball shorts. Without saying anything else I headed for the bathroom. I quickly shut the door and locked it. Knowing Janette, she may have come in here and sweet-talked her way into taking a shower together.

I turned the faucet on and splashed water on my face. I looked at my reflection in the mirror and wondered why

I was feeling so bad about this. It wasn't like it was the first time Janette and I had hooked up before. Granted, it was only once and I was drunk as hell, but I didn't feel this guilty the next day. Maybe it was the fact that Morgan was actually back in town and I knew that I still cared about her in some way. Regardless of whether she was getting married, I felt like this was wrong.

I thought all the conversations I had between Morgan, Beau, and Janette yesterday had my head spinning. I didn't know what to think about any of it. I couldn't even hear my own thoughts clearly because everybody was clouding them with theirs. This Morgan situation should not have been this complicated nor this invasive in my life. Why was I going out like this? I was a man who handled my business the way I wanted to handle it, and I thought it was about time I started acting like it. I finally came out of the bathroom and Janette was completely awake.

"So I was thinking we could go get some breakfast. I'm really in the mood for pancakes and you're all out of mix." She climbed out of bed and walked toward me. She wrapped her arms around my neck and tried to kiss me.

"Janette, we need to talk." I dodged her lips, took her hands from around my neck, and sat her on the bed.

"I thought we talked last night."

"No, you talked. Now it's my turn."

She crossed her arms and rolled her eyes. I could tell she wasn't going to be receptive to what I was about to say, but I was going to say it anyway.

"What happened last night, happened. I'm not going to say it was a mistake this time because it seemed like something we both needed. But it can't happen again."

"So we're back to Morgan now?" She got up from the edge of the bed and scrambled to find her clothes.

"This isn't about Morgan or you for that matter." I continued to watch her throw on pieces of clothing as she found them.

"Who else would it be about?" She zipped up her skirt and stormed out of the room. I followed her and watched as she tried to find her shoes in the living room.

"It's about me." Saying that statement felt cliché and kind of feminine, but it was true. "I just have a lot going on and I don't need all the extra distractions."

She finished putting on her shoes and stood up to look me straight in the eyes. I honestly couldn't tell if she was mad or upset.

"So I'm a distraction now?"

"You as well as other things." I tried to smooth things out with that line, but by the look on her face, it didn't work.

"Oh, well, that makes me feel a lot better."

She grabbed her purse off the floor and stomped past me. I grabbed her by her arm before she was able to get to the door, and stared her in her eyes. I wished I could give her something different, something that could make the situation better, but I couldn't.

"I hope you can understand."

"Oh, I understand, Henry." She snatched her arm from my grasp. "Do what you gotta do and understand that I'm gonna do the same."

She stormed out and slammed the door behind her. I had no intentions of hurting Janette, but I let out a sigh of relief. The last thing I needed to do was complicate this situation any more by being involved with Morgan's cousin. I knew they hadn't had the best relationship and I didn't want to be the reason for it becoming nonexistent.

I headed to the kitchen and made a pot of coffee. I had a feeling this was going to be a long day and I needed a boost to get me through it. I fumbled around in the refrigerator and cabinets to try to see what I could fix for breakfast. I chuckled to myself when I realized I had a taste for pancakes after all. *Maybe I should have let Janette go after we hit up IHOP.*

I could hear the faint sound of my cell phone ringing in the distance. For whatever idiotic reason, I patted the pockets on my gym shorts to see if it was there. I ran back into my bedroom and began tossing things around until I found it tangled in the sheets.

"Hello. Hello," I answered out of breath.

"Hey, Henry, this is Don."

I was excited and nervous to hear this man's voice on the other end. I calmed my breathing and gathered my thoughts before I responded. "Don, it's good to hear from you. You have any news for me?" I hated that I sounded eager but I really didn't want to make small talk. I'd waited in agony for the past few days; now, I just needed to hear the outcome.

"As a matter of fact, I do. My partners really enjoyed meeting you and after much discussion they are interested in doing business with you."

I hopped out of my bed and began to do a praise dance like old ushers do in church when they catch the Holy Spirit. I tried my best to remain quiet so that Don couldn't hear my excitement over the phone. "So I got the deal?" I finally said after I stopped dancing.

"Yup, we just gotta go over some paperwork and work out the details, but you got the deal. I'll actually be passing through this afternoon. If you want I can come by your office."

"That'll be perfect."

"Great. I'll be there around four." He hung up the phone before I could respond.

This had just become the greatest day of my life. I tried not to get my hopes up about much ever since my football career didn't work out, but I was really hoping this venture worked out. This was exactly what I needed to move to the next level and hopefully allow me to do more financially, like get my mama out of that nursing home.

I started to walk toward the bathroom to take a shower when my phone rang again. I picked up without even looking at the caller ID.

"Mission complete, bruh." I heard Beau slur through my speaker.

"Are you drunk this early in the day?" I shouldn't have been surprised that Beau had already been drinking or still drunk from whatever he got into last night. *This is why Negroes should not have days off. They don't know how to act.*

"Of course I am. It's my day off," he said, proving my point. "Besides, how else was I supposed to get the information?"

"Information about what?" I was beginning to become irritated. I didn't have time for Beau's antics today. I needed to get my mind right for this meeting with Don.

"About your competition. Morgan's fiancé comes in tomorrow at two. You still down?"

It finally dawned on me what he was talking about. I had completely forgotten about the plan to check out this dude before she brought him home. I sat on the phone, silent, contemplating if I still wanted to go through with it. *Maybe I should let this whole Morgan thing go. My business is about to really take off, I made the mistake of sleeping with her cousin, and she already told me she just wants to be friends. Maybe it isn't worth all this trouble. Maybe I should just let her get married and be happy.*

"Yo, Henry. You in or out, man?"

"I'm in. See you tomorrow."

Chapter 16

Morgan

I popped up from out my sleep and looked at the clock on my nightstand. It flashed 4:15 and I couldn't tell if it was the afternoon or the middle of the night. I remembered, vaguely, leaving the bar with Beau, and we went down to the creek and continued drinking. I didn't remember how I ended up in my bed, but I was thankful that I was here and not in a ditch somewhere. I was pretty sure Beau was the one who brought me home and placed me in my bed. *Thank God for cousins who care, even though this is kind of his fault.*

I slowly got up and stumbled my way to the bathroom. Everything in the house was blurry and I thought I was seeing double. I finally made it to my bathroom and rested here for what seemed like hours. Only when I was drunk was the restroom my favorite place to be. After sitting and taking the longest pee I thought anyone had ever taken, I got up and tried to make my way back to my room. All I wanted to do was continue to sleep this off. I was never a heavy drinker and I didn't know what made me think I could hang with Beau today. Beau had been drinking moonshine since he was seven years old. Our uncle Foot used to make it in his garage. His real name was John but everyone called him Foot because he had one foot bigger than the other, so he walked with a limp. Beau used to go to his house and help make the moonshine just so he could get a sip when it was ready. I hadn't had anything stronger than a few glasses of wine since college. Again, I didn't know why I thought I could hang with Beau.

I moved slowly along the wall to guide myself back to my room when I heard my parents arguing about something in their bedroom. I stopped and looked at my bed and debated whether I wanted to go be nosey or forget about it and crawl back into the one thing that understood me the most right now. My need to be nosey outweighed my need for recovery. I continued to creep along the wall until I reached my parents' bedroom door. I wasn't sure if they got thicker doors or my hearing was chopped and screwed because I was still drunk, but it was definitely hard to hear.

"What is the problem?" I could hear my dad say.

"The problem is that if we don't do this the right way it can backfire in our faces."

I had no idea what they were talking about but it sounded intense. I put my ear closer to the door so I could hear more.

"Juanita, maybe it's time that she knows. I mean what will it change?"

"Everything. Our whole lives that we built could turn upside down. Do you want that? Do you want to lose the one thing we were so fortunate to gain?"

A piece of me wanted to open the door and ask them what the hell they were talking about, but it was taking all my strength and energy to lean against this door. I continued to listen but certain things were muffled.

"Nita, I know we promised him, but don't you think that promise is null and void?"

"I think we should see how it plays out. We've waited this long."

My parents' back and forth was like a mental tennis match in my head. It was making me even dizzier than the tequila, but I couldn't seem to tear myself away from the door and go back to my room. What were they talking about? What promise did they make and who were they keeping something from? It sounded juicy and if I was sober I would have figured it out by now.

"Tell me what she said again," my father continued.

"She said in order for it to be executed legally, we all have to be there. All of us."

"And you are sure this is the way you want to handle it?"

The talking stopped and for a minute I thought there was something wrong with my ears. I took my ear off the door and tested them by holding my nose and humming softly. When I was satisfied, I put my ear back to the door. *I'll give it a few more seconds before I decide to finally take my butt back to my bed.*

"I think it is the way it should be handled," I finally heard my mother say.

"Okay, Juanita. This is on you. Let the record show that every time we do anything like this, I take your lead."

"Well, we have benefited from my lead so far so this time shouldn't be any different."

I felt like this conversation was winding down, and I was feeling nauseous, so I crept back to my room. I lay down on my stomach and tried to leave one foot on the floor because the room would not stop spinning. I wished I was sober so I could make sense of what my parents were talking about. Curse Beau and his bright ideas. I felt like it was something important and I needed to figure out what. Unfortunately, I was too busy trying not to vomit. Who were they talking about? What were they talking about? I wondered if there was something I could do to help. I closed my eyes and began to drift back to sleep. I hoped I could remember this tomorrow because it definitely seemed like it was important. *Lord, just make the room stop spinning.*

Chapter 17

Janette

Who did Henry think he was? First I was a mistake, now I was a distraction. None of this made any sense. I didn't think he even knew what he was doing. *I swear Morgan is a disease that is infecting my life faster than the plague. None of this would have happened if she would have kept her tail in London.* I needed to figure out how to completely get her off his mind because apparently last night wasn't enough. I felt like I had to go back to the drawing board and I hated to start over.

After leaving Henry's house in a rage, I headed home to shower and change. I didn't waste any time getting to the boutique. I needed to get my mind off of all of it: my father's death, Henry, Morgan and her poisonous existence. I figured work would be the best thing for me, especially since I hadn't been in a few days. It was the only thing I had at this point that Morgan hadn't infected.

Walking into my shop was like walking into the Twilight Zone. Everything was different. The clothes were rearranged, the sale racks were moved to different areas, there were shelves that I had never seen before, and new additions of accessories that I hadn't approved. What the hell happened while I was gone? I felt my face getting hot and I needed a target to fire a missile at. Millie walked out of the back, bopping to the music that was playing overhead.

"Oh, hey, you're back. So, what do you think?" She opened her arms like she was displaying an item on *The Price Is Right*. All I could see was red.

"Millie, what happened to my store?"

"You mean our store. And I thought it needed some new flavor so I changed it around a little."

Millie walked past me to the counter and I followed right on her heels. I wasn't in the mood for another big change in my life and I would have thought that Millie, as my best friend, would have picked up on that. The boutique was the one thing I could count on that I still had control over. I swore this week was getting worse by the minute.

"Why would you make changes to the store without talking to me first?" I crossed my arms in front of my chest and tried to stare Millie down.

She casually glanced up at me from the receipts she was separating behind the counter. "Nettie, calm down. You were going through a lot and I didn't want to bother you. Just take a look around and get acquainted with it. It's better feng shui for the atmosphere."

In what world did Millie use phrases like feng shui? Since when did she become hip to Asian practices? What was happening to my life? I went from having everything under control to it all slipping from my grasp in a matter of days. How was this even possible? I was getting angrier by the minute and I had no one to direct this energy toward. I would go off on Millie but that wouldn't help. It was Morgan who I really wanted. Ever since she showed up, everything had gone to hell in a fiery hand basket. I had to get her out of Georgia and fast.

"So did you handle it?" Millie said, looking extremely excited to hear some new gossip.

"Handle what?"

"The Henry situation. You know everyone is talking about what happened yesterday between him and Morgan. They say she might cancel the wedding so they can get back together."

I shouldn't have been surprised by that notion because that was exactly what I expected from this town, but hearing it aloud was like daggers to my soul. How dare Henry put on this big Broadway production in front of everyone? It was pissing me off that Morgan was yet again the topic of discussion.

"They are not getting back together," I snapped at Millie.

"Okay, chill. So what happened?"

I contemplated telling Millie everything about last night. How I went over to Henry's house, confronted him about Morgan, and how we made passionate love afterward. But I was not about to tell her the fiasco that happened this morning. Before I knew it, the whole town would be talking about how he dumped me and I wasn't having any of that. Henry and I were going to be together and I was prepared to do whatever it took to make sure that happened.

"Nothing happened. Henry and I are great."

Millie looked disappointed about the lack on details. "You gotta give me more than that. The last time I talked to you, you sounded like you were on a mission to shut thangs down." Millie got into her "spill the tea" pose and waited for me to give her a play-by-play.

"Just know that it's handled." I put on a fake smile and headed toward the door. "I'm gonna go grab something to eat. You want anything?"

"No," Millie said with a major attitude.

I walked out the door and quickly trotted down the street. I had to get out of there before Millie really started prying for details. I loved my best friend, but I needed to work out some kinks before I could give her a full account on Henry's and my relationship. I wasn't opposed to lying, but I needed to have a plan in place to make the overall story true.

I walked into Ray's deli a few minutes later and was immediately irritated at the line that was formed in front of the register. I hated lunch rush and I wasn't a fan of waiting, but the rumbling in my stomach forced me to stand there. I really wanted those pancakes this morning but Henry's abrupt self-realization kind of killed that dream. I shifted from side to side, trying to will the line to move faster. My patience was increasingly growing thin and I just decided to leave and grab a burger from Wendy's down the street. I turned around to walk out the door and I literally bumped into the man behind me. He was a few inches taller than me, athletic build, light skin, and beautiful green eyes. I could definitely tell he wasn't from around here.

"If the food here is that bad maybe I should consider going to wherever you were rushing off to," he said as he held on to my arm. He spoke with such professionalism in his voice, like he had been raised around rich white people his whole life. I definitely knew he wasn't from here.

"I'm sorry. I'm just not a huge fan of lines." I tried my best to match the way he spoke.

"I understand. Busy women usually don't have a lot of patience." He flashed me a smile and I could feel my knees almost give out on me. "The line is actually moving now. If you want to stay, your lunch will be my treat."

Without saying anything, I turned back around and moved forward in line. I hadn't the slightest clue who this man was, but he was intriguing and I felt like it couldn't hurt to find out. Or at least get a free lunch.

"I'm Don by the way," he whispered in my ear.

The warm, minty air from his breath against my skin made my body quiver. "Janette," I responded without turning around to face him.

"So, Janette, why is a beautiful, impatient woman like you getting her own lunch?"

"I own a boutique down the street, and I'm not getting my lunch, you are." I tried to contain my smile but I had to admit that was a good line. Even with all the Henry drama, I still possessed my flirting skills.

"Touché." He chuckled.

I finally reached the counter and ordered. I debated ordering the most expensive thing on the menu just to see how serious Mr. Don was about purchasing my food, but decided against it. I stepped aside to let him order and pay for the both of us. We walked over to a nearby table top as we waited for our orders.

"So, I assume you aren't from this neck of the woods." I couldn't stop staring into his beautiful green eyes.

"What gave it away?"

"The fact that I don't know you." He seemed to be taken aback by my response. I guessed it was the seriousness in my voice. The blessing and the curse of growing up around here was that you knew everybody, so strangers stuck out like a sore thumb.

"Do you know everyone around here?" He chuckled again.

"Just about." I kept a serious expression.

"Well, then you would be able to tell me the quickest way to HL Car Service."

The mention of Henry's business caught me off-guard. I didn't know what I expected to come out of this man's mouth but it certainly wasn't that. The wheels in my head began to turn and I was interested to see where I could take this.

"Looking to rent a limo out of town?" I wanted to be as subtle as possible.

"I actually have a business meeting with the owner."

"What business do you have with Henry?" I guessed I only knew how to be subtle for so long. Beating around the bush wasn't exactly my strong point.

"You do know everyone."

I didn't respond, just gave him a slight smile. I prompted him to continue but he hesitated for a minute to tell me anything else.

"If you must know, impatient Janette who owns a boutique down the street, we are going to start a luxury rental service in Atlanta together," he finally said.

That one statement was like hitting the lottery. My mind started working at cyber speed and I was starting to calculate my next moves. Mr. Don had provided me with all the pawns I needed to start putting this Henry train back in motion after that screeching halt he put on us this morning.

"A luxury rental service? That sounds like the worst idea I've ever heard."

Don's face was priceless. It was a mixture of being offended, shocked, and intrigued. I tried to take a mental picture so I could laugh out loud about it later.

"You know a lot about the car business?"

"I know that Atlanta is a small market. The people who are able to afford those cars either have their own to drive or have an established relationship with a rental service that already exist. It doesn't seem like a smart investment."

Don seemed to be paralyzed from what I just laid on him. I couldn't tell what he was thinking about but I knew that what I said poked at him a little. He seemed like an intelligent businessman who thoroughly thought things through, but if a consumer could plant any sort of doubt in an investor's head about losing money, they would definitely rethink their agenda. The number of my order was called and I grabbed my food. I glanced over at Don one more time as he still stood there contemplating what I just said.

"Thank you for lunch, and Henry's office is ten miles west of here."

Without waiting for a response I walked out the door and headed back to the shop. I had pep in my step and smiled with a sense of accomplishment. I felt like things were going to start going my way again. If Henry didn't want to be distracted then I would make sure that he was free of all distraction. Now I needed to set my sights on Morgan. Once she was completely out of the picture and back on that plane to London sooner rather than later, things would return to the way they were supposed to be: all about me.

Chapter 18

Morgan

My head was pounding like there were twenty little people inside it, beating against my skull with mini hammers. I didn't remember much from yesterday after I returned from the bar with Beau. Everything was a blur. I just remembered seeing flashes of my parents, food they tried to make me eat, and then me throwing up in the toilet several times. I didn't think tequila and I needed to be friends anymore because she definitely wasn't fond of me. I rolled over in my bed and cringed at the sun hitting my face. This was the worst feeling ever, and on the day I was supposed to pick up Ahvi from the airport. I was never letting Beau talk me into drinking like that again.

I glanced over at my nightstand and noticed a bottle of Advil and a glass of water resting. I slowly sat up in bed and nursed my hangover. I looked at the clock on my cell phone and was thankful it was only nine in the morning. That gave me a few hours to get myself together before I had to leave for the airport. The smell of my mother's cooking in the air compelled me to get up and head toward the kitchen to try to put something on my stomach.

"Well, look who's alive," my father said as he took a sip of his coffee.

I kissed him on the forehead and took a seat at the table. "I feel like death." I laid my head down on the table and the cool plastic placemat felt so good on my cheek.

"That's what happens when you go out foolin' with Beau." My mother set a cup of black coffee in front of me. "Drink it, you'll feel better."

I took a sip without thinking and almost burnt my tongue. As much as I hated to admit it, my mama was right. I should have never gone out drinking with Beau. Nothing I was supposed to do yesterday got accomplished. I hadn't prepared for Ahvi, I didn't write my vows, and I still didn't find out what was in that box I found under my parents' bed.

"You gon' have to get it together, baby, because we got a lot to do."

I watched as my mama hustled back and forth throughout the kitchen. It was making me dizzy all over again.

"When you get Ahvi, we gotta go over to the church and talk to Pastor Riley, we gotta swing by the floral shop to give a final say on your arrangements, and the family is having a gathering tonight so that everyone can meet your fiancé before the big day."

I quickly sobered myself up at the mention of the agenda that my mom had prepared today. I was just hoping for a calm meeting with just my parents the first night; now Ahvi had to meet my pastor and my entire family straight off the plane. My stomach dropped and I could feel the remainder of whatever was left in my system slowly creeping up. I wasn't sure I could handle all this. I wasn't sure Ahvi could handle all this. I was becoming a nervous wreck.

"Mom, don't you think that's a little overwhelming for Ahvi in one day?" I tried to figure out a way we could get rid of some of those events, like the family gathering.

"Honey, this is what happens when you throw a wedding on such short notice."

"I never wanted the wedding here to begin with." It slipped out of my mouth before I could stop myself. Both my parents looked at me like I had lost my mind. It wasn't so much what I said but the disrespectful tone that came behind that alarmed them.

"Now, your mother has been workin' hard to give you a beautiful wedding. You gon' do exactly what she says and you gon' like it." My father was stern and I felt like I was fifteen again.

"Yes, sir," was all I could respond with, for fear that I might get the life knocked out of me. I knew it didn't matter how old I was, my father would still discipline me like I was a child.

I got up from the table and proceeded back to my room. I wanted to try to sober up as much as I could before I had to pick up Ahvi. Today was going to be a long day and I needed every ounce of strength to get through it.

Hours later I awoke from my unconsciousness right in the nick of time to take a shower and be on my way. I had butterflies the whole ride to Atlanta. I was relieved that my folks went to go view my uncle's body at the funeral home instead of coming with me to the airport. I needed to see Ahvi first before my family could intervene right away.

I arrived a few minutes early and sat in front of the door where people came out of baggage claim. Usually this airport would be extremely busy but it was the middle of the week, early in the day, so I didn't have the rent-a-cops telling me I had to move my car. I stepped out of the driver's seat and walked around to lean on the hood of my car. I wanted to be sure that Ahvi saw me immediately. My legs were shaking the whole time and I tried to keep my heart rate steady. This was the moment of truth. There was no turning back once Ahvi came through those doors. I began twiddling my thumbs, trying to keep myself calm.

"Well, aren't you a vision." Ahvi's voice sounded like heaven.

I couldn't contain my excitement. I let out a loud screech and jumped into Ahvi's arms. It felt so good to be back in the presence of my love again and I planted the most passionate kiss I could muster on Ahvi's lips. "I missed you so much," I said in between kisses.

"I've missed you too." We continued our kiss for what felt like only a few seconds. I wanted to stand there and kiss on Ahvi all day, but I knew we had to finally face my family. We finally parted and I began to gather the bags from the ground.

"So have you told them yet?" Ahvi didn't waste any time as I put the luggage in the trunk.

I hesitated before I answered the question. "I couldn't bring myself to do it alone." I was too ashamed to look Ahvi in the face because I knew it had a look of disappointment on it.

"How awkward is this going to be for me?" Ahvi had always been the stronger of the two of us, so I was only thinking about how I would handle introducing Ahvi to my parents.

"What was I supposed to do?" I began to whine like a baby. Ahvi always found this annoying but it was the only tactic I had left.

"You were supposed to be honest with them."

I felt so bad having this conversation face to face. We had talked about this for a long time and I still hadn't mustered up the courage to be truthful with my parents. Now I had brought my fiancé into a very uncomfortable situation, not only with my mom and dad, but with my entire family. A tear began to roll down my face and Ahvi hugged me close and tried to console me.

"It's okay, love. I'm here now. We'll get through it together."

After a few moments of embracing, we separated from each other and proceeded to get in the car. I knew that this very long weekend was about to get even longer. The moment of truth was finally here and I had to go home and tell my family that the man I was in love with and was planning on spending the rest of my life with was a woman.

Chapter 19

Henry

I knew I said I was up for scoping out the competition but I was not in the mood for it today. Yesterday went from the worst to the best back to the worst day of my life. I thought everything was in order for my deal with Don until he came to my office unsure about the investment. He was going on and on about how he wasn't sure if it was the right thing to do and he needed more time to look at everything. I couldn't understand it. When I spoke with him over the phone he seemed excited about the venture and ready to work with me. I didn't know what changed his mind from that phone call to the office meeting. Now Beau and I were sitting at the airport like some undercover detective agents, looking for a dude we had never seen before.

Beau got us to the airport around one-thirty just to make sure we had enough time to see everything go down. I swore this man seemed more excited to do this than I was. He had on all black with a scully hat and some "too dark to see your eyeballs" shades. In this heat, I was surprised this fool didn't burst into flames.

"You see her yet?" he asked as he pulled out a pair of binoculars.

I couldn't help but to laugh out loud.

"Are you serious with this stuff?" I continued to laugh as Beau struggled with the binoculars and his sunglasses all at the same time.

"What? This is proper stakeout attire."

"But this isn't a stakeout, dude." I was laughing so hard tears began to roll down my face. Even if I never saw Morgan's fiancé, watching Beau make a complete fool out of himself was well worth the trip.

"Whatever, man. I'm just tryin'a make sure Morgan doesn't recognize me."

"Beau, we are in an unmarked car with tinted windows. Nobody is going to recognize you." I finally slowed my laughter down to a chuckle and tried to breathe normally. This had to be the worst mission Beau and I had ever tried to accomplish. I was seventy-three percent sure Beau was still drunk from yesterday.

We waited in silence for a few moments and then saw Morgan pull past us in her mother's car. Both of us slumped down in our seats in a panic to make sure she didn't see us. My heart was beating fast again and I realized that I was interested in seeing this dude. I had been going back and forth in my mind about spying, but I needed to see what he had that I didn't. I wanted to see what Morgan thought was so special about this man that she would actually go through with marriage.

I saw her get out of the car and lean up against the hood on the passenger side. She looked so beautiful. The jean shorts she wore hugged her curves like they were holding on for dear life. The cutoff she had on showed the belly button piercing she got our junior year. I remembered the day we went to the tattoo parlor after my grandma died. It was her way of cheering me up. It probably wasn't the best way to cheer me up because that tattoo hurt like hell, but I loved her effort. It was little things like that that made me realize at a young age how special she was to me. I definitely had to see what I was up against.

"She looks nervous," Beau said, peering at her through those ridiculous binoculars.

"So?" I slapped the binoculars out of his hands. He looked at me like we were about to scuffle but he knew better. He may have been four inches taller than me but he could never handle me when it came to fighting. All his life I'd told him football players were tougher than basketball players. We got hit for a living.

"So it may mean she's having second thoughts."

"Or it may mean she's nervous about seeing her fiancé for the first time in almost a week. Do you have to overanalyze everything?"

I darted my eyes back and forth between Morgan and the door. I never watched something so intensely before in my life. I kept imagining this Idris Elba–looking dude come out the door and sweep her off her feet. My phone buzzed and I looked down at it to see a text message from Janette. I quickly ignored and looked back up at the door. I was immediately struck by the beauty of a woman walking out into the sun. She was at least five foot ten, with short, sandy blond hair that was slicked back. She had this exotic look to her like she was mixed with something that I couldn't put my finger on. I told myself if Morgan really ended up married, I would track this girl down and make her my plan B. I watched her walk all the way up to Morgan and stop. It wasn't until I saw Morgan leap into her arms that I finally realized what was going on.

"Oh, hell naw. She left you for a woman?" Beau yelled as we both saw Morgan and the gorgeous woman engage in a long kiss.

I couldn't believe what I was seeing. This couldn't be real. Morgan was engaged to a woman? This had to be a joke. Maybe this was Ahvi's sister and this was just how they said hello in Europe. I never even knew Morgan liked women, let alone planned on marrying one.

"Yo. Henry. Are you seeing this?" Beau exclaimed.

"Yes, idiot, I see it. I'm not blind," I snapped at Beau before I realized it. I was still in utter shock at what I was witnessing.

"Ay, don't take your frustrations out on me 'cause you got dumped by a lesbian."

I wanted to smack him in the back of his head, but he was right. I didn't know what to do about this situation. I didn't know many lesbians, especially ones I had dated previously. Only time I ever saw two women together was on the Internet, or a couple of times back in the day on away games, but they were usually with me, too.

"She is fine though," Beau continued. "I would leave you for her too."

"She didn't leave me for her." I tried to convince myself that this didn't have anything to do with me, but it was hard to digest. All I could think about was me driving her to the point where she no longer wanted to deal with men.

"So what are you gonna do? The way I see it, you either ask to join the party or give up. 'Cause it ain't no way you can compete with another woman. Especially not one as fine as that."

I continued to watch the two of them in silence. For a moment it looked like they were arguing. I saw Ahvi grab Morgan close to her and wipe away tears. This was an unreal sight. The only woman I had ever loved was in love with another woman. For most men this would be a fantasy come true, but for me this was a stab in the heart. Beau had a point. Another man I could try to compete with, but a woman? How was I supposed to change someone's sexual orientation? I watched as they got in the car and drove away. Beau and I both still sitting there in shock.

"Sooo, that was interesting," Beau joked, trying to break the awkward silence.

I was unable to form words. There weren't too many times in my life that I'd been speechless but this was definitely in the top five. I couldn't speak. I couldn't move. I was surprised that I was still breathing.

"If you don't say something sometime soon, I'm gonna take you over to sixth ward and get you checked out."

"Morgan is a lesbian," I finally said.

"I think we established that five minutes ago when she was slobbin' down that model."

"Morgan is a lesbian?" I ignored what Beau was saying and tried to gather my thoughts. Those were the only four words I could put together to make a sentence. Maybe if I constantly said it out loud it would begin to make sense.

"Okay, you're scaring me now. What do you want me to do? You want me to go after them or head back home?"

I didn't know how Beau was more cool, calm, and collected than me. I guessed since it was his cousin, it really didn't matter to him either way.

"Go home. I've seen enough for today."

Beau turned the ignition and sped off toward the highway. The whole ride home, I replayed the scene from the airport over and over again in my head, from the time I saw them kissing to the time they left. Things just didn't add up. How could Morgan be a lesbian? I mean, she'd had sex with me. I didn't mean to brag but that alone should have been enough to keep her on this team. I needed to get answers on how this happened. There was no way she was going to be able to go through with the ceremony here in Georgia, so that gave me time to confront her. None of this made any sense. *Morgan is a lesbian?*

Chapter 20

Janette

Viewing my daddy's body was probably the hardest thing I ever had to do in my life. I had never even seen a dead body before, so for the first one to be my dad was excruciating. My mama was a complete wreck. Every few minutes she would let out this bone-shattering cry and it made me break down even more. My brother was rubbing her back the whole time, trying to be strong and hold back his tears, but I could tell he was devastated. This whole situation was unreal. I didn't want to believe that my father was no longer with us. All I wanted him to do was to pop up out of that box and tell us he was joking. Tell us that he lost a bet and took it too far. Anything would be better than the reality of him being dead.

"Does he look like how you remembered him?" This short, bald-headed man I had never seen before finally said.

"The last time I saw my father, he was alive. So, hell no, he doesn't look like the way we remember him." Everybody looked at me like I had lost my mind. My heart was so broken I didn't even realize I had disrespected the room.

"Janette Marie Maxson, you mind your tongue. How dare you speak like that?" My mother wiped her tears and straightened up to discipline me.

"I'm sorry, Mama." I lowered my eyes in shame. Though I had my daddy's mouth, I knew he wouldn't want me to talk like that, especially in front of my mama.

"He looks fine, Fred. Thank you," my mother said to the short man. "Do you think we can have a few moments alone with him?"

Fred nodded his head and backed out of the room. JJ and I made eye contact with each other, both unsure about our mama's next move. She walked up to my father slowly and stood at his head. My brother and I moved closer to each other and held hands. My mother caressed my father's face and began humming his favorite song. Watching her straighten his clothes like she used to do before he would leave the house was endearing and painful at the same time.

"May we come in?" My aunt Beanie poked her head around the door. She walked in the room without waiting for anyone to respond and immediately went to my mama's side. I watched as they embraced and cried together. I knew this was just as painful for my aunt Beanie as it was for my mother. My daddy and his baby sister had always been close, and for as long as I could remember, they always seemed to have this special bond that only they understood. It was like they went through something important together and shared a secret.

"We all gonna miss him," I heard Beanie whisper in my mama's ear.

I could feel my eyes welling up again and I didn't want to endure another round of uncontrollable crying. I decided to step out the room and let them have their moment. I ran into my uncle Earl in the lobby and sat next to him in the waiting area. We sat side by side in silence, staring out into space. I had no idea what to say and he looked like he couldn't form the words to say anything.

"You don't want to go see Daddy?" I finally said, breaking our silence.

He shifted in his seat and dropped his eyes to the floor. I could see pain and heartache rush through his whole body. He cleared his throat almost like he was choking back tears. "I've held death in my hands one time in my life and I knew I never wanted to get that close to it again." He quickly swatted a tear from the corner of his eye.

"You've held death in your hands?" I had no clue why it intrigued me to hear this story, but the urge was inexplicably strong. He hesitated for a brief moment, contemplating whether he really wanted to tell me his experience.

"When Beanie and I were first married we lost a son."

I tried my best to hide my shock but my mouth inadvertently dropped. I had never heard this before, and living in this town, news like that tended to be repeated. "Aunt Beanie had a miscarriage?" I tried to sound less nosey and more sympathetic.

"No, she had him but there were a lot of complications during labor. I almost lost both of them."

I could see him reliving the incident in his mind. My uncle Earl had always been such a big family man. I couldn't imagine how difficult that situation must have been for him. I tried to find appropriate words to say, but decided to remain quiet.

"He lived two hours and thirty-seven minutes," he continued. "He took his last breath in the palm of my hands. Beanie never even got to see him."

I had so many questions I wanted to ask. So many things I wanted to know. How did no one know about this? Why was this a huge secret around town? I mean, a miscarriage you can conceal, but a full-term pregnancy and then no baby was something that people around here would definitely talk about. Was it around the time Morgan was born? Was she even their daughter or was she a replacement baby for the one they lost? Was that

the reason they treated her like a china doll? So many
thoughts swam in my head, but I knew asking them
at this moment would be completely inappropriate. I
planned to find out though.

We sat in an awkward silence once again when I saw JJ
come down the hall.

"Is Mama ready to go?" I asked before he could come
sit next to me.

"Naw, Beanie needed to talk to her for a moment."

JJ sat down and the three of us stared into space
without a peep out of any of us. I wondered what my
mama and Beanie were talking about. I wondered if I was
going to find out more about the story Uncle Earl just told
me. I wondered if JJ knew. With all of this going on, my
mind was completely off my father's death, the issue with
Henry, and Morgan's wedding. I was actually thankful for
the distraction.

A few minutes later my mother stormed down the
hallway and out the door with tears in her eyes. Without
thinking, JJ and I jumped up and followed her out. It
wasn't like my mom to ever just leave abruptly.

"Mama, what happened?" I asked as soon as we all
were in the car.

"Nothing, just tired and ready to go home."

Without any hesitation, JJ put the car in drive and sped
off. He wasn't the type to question anything. If Mom said
she was tired, she was tired, and that was the end of it. For
me, I needed to know what happened. Nothing about this
day felt right and I needed to figure out why. What did my
aunt say? What were they hiding? Something was going on
and I didn't plan to stand around and wait to be blindsided.
I sat back in my seat and began to come up with a plan.

Chapter 21

Morgan

Every fiber in my body tingled. On one hand I was so excited to see Ahvi and be back with her; on the other I was deathly terrified of presenting her to my family. I knew this day would come eventually, but I could admit that I didn't think this whole scenario through. Why did I agree to do this? We couldn't even legally get married in Georgia.

"Morgan, your thoughts are hurting me," Ahvi said as she tried to pry her hand from my kung fu grip I didn't realize I had on her.

"I'm sorry, babe." I let go of her and grabbed the wheel at a ten-and-two position.

"I know you're nervous, but I think it's about time that your parents find out." Ahvi's voice was soothing but not to the point where I was calm about this. Coming out to my parents was definitely on my biggest fears list.

"So what am I supposed to do? Just walk in there and say, 'Hey, Mom and Dad. Remember the man you thought I was going to marry? Well he is actually a she. Welcome her to the family.'" I could feel that my sarcasm was a little rough, but this was an intense situation that I wasn't prepared for.

Ahvi sat back in her seat and folded her arms. It was a look she always gave when she waited for me to realize that I was wrong. I hated that look.

"I'm sorry," I said as I grabbed her hand and kissed the back of it. "I don't think I handled this situation properly and I'm scared it is about to be a major disaster."

"Granted, you should have told them a long time ago and this will probably be very uncomfortable, but they are your parents and they love you and they will come to accept it."

She pulled my hand toward her lips and began to softly kiss up and down my arm. It sent a chill up my spine and put a smile on my face. I truly did love this woman. She knew every way to balance me out.

"Besides," she continued, "I will be brilliant and charming and they will love me regardless."

"I hope so, because we're here." I pulled up to the house and recognized about ten cars in the driveway. My mother had already organized a party with family and probably a few of her friends. I contemplated putting the car in reverse and driving anywhere, but Ahvi hopped out like she was going to an amusement park for the first time.

"Let's go." She came around to the driver's side and pulled me out of the car. Each step toward the door felt like my final walk down the green mile. I began to take deep breaths to calm my nerves but it wasn't working. I was terrified. I grabbed Ahvi's hand and held it close. I needed to feel her touch in order for me not to turn around and run down the street.

"Surprise," everyone yelled in our direction as we walked through the door.

I thought it was kind of comical seeing as everyone's car was completely visible. I felt the energy in the room go from excited to confused. Everyone's eyes felt like they were burning a hole right through my soul. My mother walked over to me with that smile that Southern women put on to not give away that something is wrong.

"Honey, where is Ahvi?" she tried to whisper to me.

I looked around at my family, who was staring at me, waiting for an explanation. I squeezed Ahvi's hand a little tighter and I could feel her squeeze back, giving me the okay to tell them the truth.

"Everyone, this is Ahvi."

My mother's face turned to stone and I heard gasps of shock around the room.

"Oh hell, she done switched to the other side," I heard my boisterous cousin Yolanda yell out.

"Hi." Ahvi stuck her hand out and my mother just stood there motionless. I wanted to say something to ease the situation, but I was afraid that if I made any sudden movements, she would backhand me.

"Maybe we should talk in private." My father came up behind my mother to prevent any sort of a scene.

Ahvi and I began to follow my parents to their room.

"Just the three of us," he said as he turned around abruptly and stopped Ahvi in her tracks. I was concerned about leaving her alone with my family, but she nodded that she would be fine by herself.

I stepped into my parents' room and immediately sat on the bed while my mother paced back and forth. I had never seen her like this. There wasn't much that I did growing up to render a reaction like this so I wasn't sure what to expect.

"Explain to me what I just saw out there," she finally said. I was about to open my mouth to speak when she continued. "I mean this is a joke, right?"

I waited a few minutes to see if she was going to say something else. When she didn't, I tried to find the words to explain it to them.

"I know this is a shock, but I am in love." I was hoping that would hit a soft spot with them but apparently it made them more upset.

"I can't even express what I'm feeling right now because I know this isn't the child I raised."

I sat there like a twelve-year-old as my mother struggled to comprehend what was happening. I found my thoughts drifting to Ahvi in the room with my family. I hoped she wasn't being interrogated like I was.

"Are you listening to me?" my mother yelled, snapping me back to the present moment.

"Okay, why don't we take a step back. Morgan, how long have you been . . ."

"A lesbian?" I finished the question for my father. My mother almost had a heart attack at the mention of the word. I thought being delicate with my family was the way to go, but all I wanted to do was get out there with my fiancé. "Listen, guys, I love you both and I respect you, but this is who I am and I am going to marry her."

I shocked myself with how bold I was with them. I had never talked to them so matter-of-factly, but this situation wasn't going to get any better if I tiptoed around it.

"How do you think you are going to get married here in Georgia? We are supposed to meet with the reverend tomorrow." My mother looked like she was on the brink of tears.

I wished I could say something to comfort her, but there was probably nothing I could say that would help unless it was, "April Fools.'"

"I don't know, Mom, because we had planned to get married in Spain." I was over this conversation at this point. I was glad that everything was out in the open but having a wedding in Georgia was not my concern. "Guys, why don't you just meet her and we can talk about this later."

Without waiting for a response I got up from the bed and left the room. I wasn't going to be held hostage any longer and I wanted to make sure that my family hadn't slaughtered Ahvi and were beginning to pick at her bones.

When I walked into the living room, my little cousins were all over her. I couldn't tell whether they were interested in her until I saw Ahvi burst into laughter.

"So you never been with a man before?" I heard my cousin Jayla ask as I got closer to them.

"Once, when I was fourteen. I dated Arthur Wells, but he now lives with his boyfriend in France," she responded. The teenagers seemed so fascinated with her, which warmed my heart a little. I was glad to see someone was on my side.

"Okay, everyone, stand down." I squeezed between Ahvi and one of my cousins on the couch and placed a soft kiss on her cheek. I could feel the stares from around the room.

"Where's your loo?" I had a feeling that the stares were a little uncomfortable for Ahvi as well and she needed to regroup. I gave her the directions to the bathroom and watched as she switched down the hall. As soon as she closed the door I was bombarded with questions. It seemed like everyone in the room had something to say or ask and it all sounded like German coming at me.

"Everybody, listen up." My father's voice was commanding and quieted the room. "We are going to treat Ahvi with respect, get to know her, and nobody is going to embarrass Morgan."

My daddy's statement had me speechless. I was shocked and elated that they were going to support me. I got up from the couch and jumped in his arms like I was five years old. I didn't know why but I was happy that my parents decided to accept not only me, but Ahvi. It made me reconsider my feelings about this weekend.

"We're going to finish our conversation later," he whispered in my ear. His tone wasn't as accepting as it was a second ago. Maybe I got excited too early.

Everybody began to gravitate toward the dining room to eat and I was left standing there to prepare myself for what this weekend was really going to bring. I was praying that I could get through the rest of this trip with Ahvi by my side, but I had a feeling it wasn't going to be all acceptance and roses.

Chapter 22

Henry

I was still utterly confused by what we saw at the airport when we pulled up to Morgan's engagement party a few hours later. Morgan, the woman I had known my whole life, was planning on marrying a woman. Granted, she was a very fine woman, but how was this possible? I mean, I didn't care how good-looking Idris Elba was to women around the world, dude ain't fine enough to turn me gay. I questioned myself the whole ride back. Did I do something to turn her off men? Was Ahvi the first girl she'd been with? Was my sex bad? What was I saying? Of course my sex wasn't bad. Morgan may have been my first but I was a natural in them sheets.

"Are you sure you tryin'a do this?" Beau asked, pulling me out of my thoughts. He shut the car off and stared at the house as if it were possessed. "I mean, we can go hit the bar right now and forget we know anything."

I didn't even ponder over that option like I normally would. I wanted to go in here and figure out how this was even possible. I wanted to know if this had something to do with me. I got out of the car without answering Beau. I could hear him scrambling behind me to get out of the car and catch up. I was intently focused on getting inside the house and talking to Morgan.

"Last chance, bruh. We don't have to do this." Beau made his final plea as we reached the porch.

I knew that whatever he said wouldn't sway me. "Beau, chill. Go in here, eat some food, kick it with your fam, and let me do what I gotta do."

I walked into the house and it wasn't the same vibe that most Willis gatherings had. People were mingling and eating, but there was an awkward tension in the air. It felt like everyone was tiptoeing around an enormous elephant in the room. I spotted Morgan in the kitchen with the woman we saw her pick up from the airport. She had a look in her eyes that I had never seen before. She gazed at this woman with so much passion, it almost made me turn around and leave.

"Hey, everybody." I received several different reactions as I announced myself. I could tell some people were happy to see me, some people were wondering what I was doing there, and some people wanted to see if there were going to be fireworks. I was actually grateful that Beau talked me in to going to the airport to see Ahvi before anyone else because I couldn't imagine walking into this situation blindly.

"Y'all didn't eat all the food, did you?" Beau said, being his normal greedy self. It actually relieved some of the tension and turned the focus off me. I made my way to the kitchen while Beau was being a diversion. Watching the two of them sneak kisses and play and laugh with each other reminded me when we were sixteen. It gave me a lump in my throat and a pain in my gut. Maybe it's true what they say: you never forget your first.

"Am I interrupting something?" I said, kind of startling them. They separated quickly as if they just got caught by their parents.

"Henry, I wasn't expecting to see you today."

"And miss one of your mom's parties? Never." The three of us stood there in silence for a moment. Morgan looked like she didn't know what to say and Ahvi stood there awkwardly, waiting to be introduced.

"I'm Ahvianna." The gorgeous woman from the airport extended her hand. She was even more beautiful up close and I could see the appeal, but it still didn't explain to me Morgan wanting to marry this woman.

"I'm sorry. Henry, this is my fiancé, Ahvi. Ahvi, this is Henry. We grew up together."

I shook Ahvi's hand and was completely offended with the comment Morgan just made. *We grew up together? Oh, I see what time it is.* If she wanted to play this game, I knew how to beat her.

"Well, we did a little more than just grow together." I gave a sly smirk and I could tell it rubbed Morgan the wrong way. "Can we talk?" I turned my attention back to Morgan.

"I don't think that's—"

"Oh, Ahvi doesn't mind, do you?" I quickly cut off her resistant rant that she was about to get into.

"Of course not. I'll just go help myself to some more food." She kissed Morgan on the cheek and walked out the kitchen.

We stared at each other, both refusing to break eye contact.

"What do you want, Henry?" she finally said with an attitude that I thought we had gotten past.

"I'm here to congratulate the happy couple."

"Oh, please, you are not. I know you better than that."

This argument seemed so familiar. It was starting to feel like our comfort zone. We couldn't have a conversation like normal adults.

"Oh right, because we grew up together." I hated to recycle lines but I knew that it would get to her as much as it got to me.

"I'm not having this conversation with you at my engagement party." She tried to walk past me but I grabbed her arm. She wasn't going to play me like I didn't matter just because she was hitting for a different team now.

"Yes, you are. Out of all the things we've been through, you owe me this conversation."

Morgan was good for standing toe to toe with me in an argument but I wanted her to know that I wasn't backing down. She was famous for running away from her problems, so it was way overdue for her to face them head-on. I was going to get an answer out of her today. She snatched away from me and opened the back door for me to follow her out.

"So Ahvi is a woman? How long were you going to keep that a secret?" I said as we got out to the back porch.

"Forever if I could've."

She tried to sound sarcastic but I could tell she was serious. I knew this was not something Morgan wanted any of us to know. "See, now that's what I don't understand. Aren't you supposed to tell everyone about the person you are going to spend the rest of your life with?"

"What do you really want?"

"How long have you known that you were gay?" I could feel myself getting heated. I didn't want to be a punk and make a scene, but this was really affecting me.

"Why does it matter?" She began to raise her voice and I wasn't going to be intimidated.

"Because as the man who was in love with you for his whole life, I need to know."

She got really quiet and I was a little afraid of what was going through her head.

"If I tell you the truth will you be satisfied?" she said in a calm tone. The switch was a little eerie for me and I wasn't sure if I wanted her to answer the question.

"Yeah, I'll drop it," I said without thinking.

"I was twelve when I knew I was attracted to girls. I had my first kiss with one at Mallory Jones's slumber party for her thirteenth birthday. I fooled around with girls all through high school and had my first real girlfriend during my second semester of freshmen year at NYU. So to answer your question, I've basically known my whole life."

I was completely flabbergasted at the proclamation she just made to me. You would have thought the woman that you loved liking girls would be a sexy thing, but it was like daggers to my heart. Every word she spoke in her little soliloquy felt like I was being hit in the gut repeatedly by Floyd Mayweather.

"So what were we? Your cover?" I hated that I sounded like a female, but those were the only words that would come out my mouth.

"Henry, I was trying to figure myself out. I figured if the greatest guy in the whole town couldn't get my mind off women, then no one could."

"Wow, well, I'm glad to know that when I was loving you, you were using me to make yourself straight." I tried my hardest to control my emotions. I couldn't tell if I was sad, mad, upset, or hurt, and that was pissing me off. I could feel my eyes welling up and I quickly looked away from Morgan to pull myself together.

"You and I will forever be connected because you are my first and only guy. You will always have a special place in my heart because of that."

"Well, I see what you meant when you said Ahvi has things I don't have."

I wanted to pick my next words very carefully because I knew this may be the last time I ever spoke to Morgan. I used to hate watching those sappy chick flicks, like *The Notebook,* with women I would date. There was always some point in the movie where the main couple would break up and one of the characters would make this big good-bye speech that left the women who were watching it crying. I always thought scenes like that were completely fictional and would never happen in real life.

Apparently I was wrong because this seemed like one of those scenes. I was the one who was about to make the sappy good-bye speech.

"I want you to know that you were never just some girl I grew up with. I was honest when I said I saw myself with you for the rest of my life. I wish you would've been honest with me."

I leaned over to her and kissed her softly on the cheek. I felt a tear fall from her eye land on my face. I wrapped my arms around her waist and held her for the last time. I could feel her heart beating fast and I knew we were in a consensus that this would be our last encounter.

"Henry, I never meant to hurt you. I need you to believe that. I really do love you, just not like I love Ahvi."

She tried to sound comforting, but her words stung like a thousand wasps. I never thought this was how it would end between us. Hell, I honestly never thought we would ever be over. I always thought Morgan and I would eventually find our way back to each other.

"Best of luck with the marriage," I said as I pulled away from her embrace. I took a final look at her face and then proceeded to walk around the house. I didn't want to go back to the party and pretend like I was over it. I walked down the road, not knowing exactly where I was headed. The only thing I could think about was how grateful I was that the sun was setting, and how I needed a stiff drink.

Chapter 23

Janette

I couldn't get the scene at the funeral home out of my head. Everything about this morning was so awkward. I really wanted to get more information about what Uncle Earl said about them losing a son. It was so unlikely for something like that to be unknown, at least to the family. My mama was acting weird as well. Storming out the building without any explanation and locking herself in her room was so unlike her. I tried a couple of times to check on her and get her something to eat but she refused to open the door. I decided to stay at my parents' house to keep an eye on her.

I spent most of the day on my computer, trying to see if I could pull up any newspaper articles or documents of a couple losing a baby. I Googled everything I could think of but came up empty. There had to be something I could find about this.

"Hey, you're still here," JJ said as he stood in my doorway.

"Yeah, I wanted to stick around in case Mom wanted to talk. Where you been?" I realized I hadn't seen my brother since we got back to the house.

"Had to go spend time with Paula. You know her, she's only understanding for so long before she starts complaining."

I hated my brother's girlfriend. He met her a few years ago at a car and bike show in Atlanta and they had been on and off ever since. I always looked at her as someone who wanted a man to take care of her. Now that I thought about it, I didn't know why I hadn't tried to get rid of her by now. *After this weekend is over, I may need to make that my next project.*

"Have you ever heard anything about Uncle Earl and Beanie losing a son?" I wasn't going to even acknowledge the Paula comment.

"Naw, how did you hear about it?" He looked just as confused as I did this morning.

"Uncle Earl told me himself today. I just thought it was weird that we've never heard about it before."

"Well, that's not something people want to be spread around." As quickly as he was confused, he was uninterested. JJ was never one for gossip and he tried to stay out of people's drama. That was so odd to me.

"I know, but isn't it strange that there has never been any mention about it?"

"Nettie, I don't know what you are fishing for, but let it go. People lose children all the time and it's not something they want to talk about." He gave me a reassuring kiss on my forehead as he always did. "I'm tired and I'm going to bed."

He walked out the room and I took in a deep breath. Maybe he was right. Maybe I was over-thinking things. I needed to relax. This whole week so far was really getting to me. I shut my computer and lay back on my bed. I gazed at my ceiling and began to think about my daddy. I had been distracted lately and hadn't really harped on the memories I had with him. The times I most remembered having with my father was playing chess with him. He would teach me life lessons and strategy.

"Always look at things from every angle. You never want to be without a plan B," he would say as he moved pieces around the board.

I never realized how much he shaped me. I closed my eyes and felt a tear fall down my cheek. I missed him. An annoying buzz coming from my back pocket yanked me out of my moment. I pulled out my phone and quickly answered it without looking at who it was.

"Girl, I hope you are sitting down for this one." Millie's voice blared through the phone.

"I'm not really in the mood for gossip, Mills." For once I was going to take my brother's advice and let things go. I just wanted to focus on my business tonight.

"If you don't want to hear how Morgan's future husband is actually a woman, then I'll just call somebody who does."

I sat straight up in the bed. This must have been a dream. There was no way I heard what I thought I just heard. Morgan "Miss Perfect" Willis was a lesbian?

"Say what now?" was all that could come out my mouth.

"Girl, I heard she walked into her engagement party with this tall, exotic, model-looking woman and said that she was Ahvi."

My jaw hit the floor. I had heard a lot of juicy gossip over the years and had seen some unbelievable things, but nothing seemed to top this news. I couldn't even find the words to respond.

"Then," Millie continued, "Henry showed up and they had this big argument in the backyard and he stormed off."

My heart dropped at the mention of Henry's name. Why were they still doing the Morgan-Henry tango? I was hoping that he had gotten past that stage already.

"Where is he?" I finally spoke.

"Nobody knows. They said Beau has been calling him and looking for him, but hasn't had any luck."

I took a moment to think about all the places he would go after a scene like that. His office and house had probably already been checked. I got up from my bed and grabbed my shoes when it hit me.

"Uh, hello? I'm still here."

"I'm gonna call you back." I could only imagine the shock and disappointment on her face. I knew she wanted me to be more reactive, but I had a different plan in mind. I hung up the phone without saying another word and rushed out the house. I was surprised I even managed to grab my wallet and my keys before I hit the door.

I took a drive about twenty miles outside of town to where I thought Henry would be. There was a bar he frequented when he didn't want to run into anyone he knew. It was the place we drank at the first night we hooked up. I spotted him from the front door sucking down what looked like Hennessy and then motioned to order another.

"Make that two," I said to the bartender as I sat down next to Henry.

"Fancy meeting you here," he said through a drunken chuckle. "You a detective now?"

"Trust me, honey, I could've found Osama bin Laden if I wanted it bad enough." The bartender brought us our drinks and I quickly threw it back like a shot and ordered another one.

"I'm guessing you heard the truth about Ahvi." He took a sip of his drink and I could see him swallowing his pain.

"Yeah, I did." I wanted to comfort him without seeming pushy so I didn't say too much. "Are you okay?"

"Oh, that was good." He chuckled again. "That almost sounded like you genuinely care."

I was a little taken aback by his comment. I knew he was hurting but I wasn't going to be his punching bag. I didn't see Morgan out looking for him, hoping he was okay.

"I do genuinely care." I tried to touch his hand and he picked up his drink. I tried not to trip and followed suit with the fresh drink that was placed in front of me.

"You are elated that there is no possible way Morgan would want to get back with me and you are here to capitalize."

"That is not true." I really was being sincere. It was beginning to piss me off that he couldn't see that.

"Then why are you here, Janette?"

"I felt like you needed a drinking partner with the week you have had. Between your business venture kind of falling through and Morgan being a lesbian, I—"

"Wait, what did you just say?" He cut me off in mid-sentence and I scrambled to try to remember what just came out of my mouth. "How do you even know about my business venture?"

My stomach quickly fell to my feet and I immediately knew I messed up. How did I just put my foot in my mouth trying to be genuine?

"You know how people talk. I heard it around." I tried to clean it up as much as I could, but even in his intoxicated state, I could tell, he wasn't buying it.

"No one knew about that deal so I'm going to ask you again. How did you know?"

I could see his anger building inside of him and it was a bit intimidating. I made that move to help my chances with Henry, not to sabotage them. I tried to think of a lie to cover my tracks but the two drinks were kicking in and I could feel the truth seeping out.

"I may have run into Don earlier this week." It was almost like I couldn't stop it from coming out. I looked straight in Henry's face and it seemed like I could see steam coming out his ears.

"What the hell did you do?"

The way he looked at me was something I had never seen before. It was almost like pure disgust and hatred and I had no idea what to say to diffuse the situation. I hated resorting to the truth if I had no clue if it was going to be in my favor.

"I simply made a suggestion and—"

He jumped off the barstool before I could finish telling him what happened. He looked at me like I was a ghost who was haunting him. "I knew something interfered and I couldn't figure out what. It was you."

"Henry, I didn't mean to hurt you." I got up from my seat and tried to go to him but he swatted me away.

"All the women in your family are toxic. I don't know what I did to have you try to ruin my life, but I want you and your carpet-munching cousin to stay far away from me." He dug in his pocket and pulled out money and threw it on the bar.

I had never seen Henry like this and I felt bad that I contributed to his outburst. He stumbled out of the door and I was left standing there trying to comprehend what just happened. I really wished my daddy was here at this moment to tell me what to do because I didn't have a plan B.

Chapter 24

Morgan

If I had to delete any day out of my entire life, yesterday would have definitely been that day. I was glad everything was out in the open but I could have done without the drama. My family was on the best possible behavior they could've been on but the vibe was awkward and uncomfortable. My cousins wouldn't stop asking Ahvi lesbian questions as if they were researching her for a school project. My mom was quiet the entire time, and that conversation with Henry was the most difficult one I ever had in my life. I worried about him the entire night and tried to find out where he stormed off to.

The worst part of the night was the continuation of the discussion my parents and I started in their room. This time they wanted to include Ahvi and get to the bottom of how this union even happened. I felt like we murdered someone and they were trying to get a confession out of us. They didn't even allow Ahvi to sleep in my room. She was banished to the basement. My father made it a point to express just how uncomfortable he was with me sharing a bed with another woman under his roof. At this point I was counting down the days until we returned to our peaceful home in London. If I was lucky my parents would forget the whole thing and we could be out of here quicker.

My mother was still adamant about going to meet with her pastor this morning. I didn't know what today was going to bring but I definitely knew it wasn't going to be good. *A black Southern preacher talking to two lesbians about their wedding plans? You can't even make that up in a Tyler Perry movie.*

I tiptoed around my room and the bathroom, trying to make the least amount of noise possible so I wouldn't have to have an early-morning conversation with my parents. I didn't know how much more lecturing and questions I could take from them.

I walked into the kitchen and to my surprise everyone was dressed and eating breakfast silently. I could tell my parents were completely out of their element and didn't know what else to do or say. It was never this quiet at our breakfast table. I could only imagine how Ahvi was feeling right now. Maybe I should have just ignored my mother's request to come out here and stayed where we were safe and comfortable.

"Morning." I tried to sound enthusiastic but nobody even made an attempt. I got no response. I grabbed a piece of toast off the counter and tried to stuff my face before anyone changed their mind about staying silent.

"Well, I gotta go check on the shop." My father got up from the table and placed his dishes in the sink without even looking at me. It was the first time he had given me the silent treatment and it was a crushing blow. We had always been close and he always had my back in most of the decisions I had made, so for him to be completely disappointed in me really hurt.

"See you later, baby," he said as he kissed my mother on her forehead. He headed out the door without even looking back or saying good-bye to me and I could feel the tears coming. I turned toward the sink so that no one could see them fall, and tried my best to straighten up my face. I didn't know what I expected their reaction to be but I definitely didn't think that my dad would actually stop talking to me. I knew he would be disappointed, but I had hoped that he loved me enough to move past it and be there for me.

My mother followed my father's lead and got up from the table to place her dishes in the sink. I wiped my face and sniffled so that she couldn't see me crying.

"I'm going to be ready to go in about ten minutes. Will you be ready by then?"

"Yes, ma'am," were the only words that I could respond with. If I had said anything else I felt like I would be a puddle on the floor.

She walked out of the kitchen and I almost fell to my knees. I felt Ahvi quickly come behind me to catch me before I hit the floor. I turned toward her and buried my face in her chest. I couldn't control my emotions anymore and I began to weep.

"It's okay. Coming out is hard, especially in these circumstances. I'm sure they'll come around sooner or later."

"And if they don't?" I said with my head still laid on her. She lifted my head and kissed my tears on my cheek, which made me smile.

"Then I will whisk you away to a lovely chateau in Paris and we can do this the right way."

Ahvi's comment made me grin from ear to ear and it reminded me that I was one-hundred percent happy with my decision to be with her. She was my other half and I was grateful for her. I kissed the inside of her hands and took a deep breath to calm myself.

"Let's go finish getting ready." I let go of her hands and walked back to my room to gather my things. The last thing I wanted was my mother to be mad about not leaving on time on top of everything else.

As soon as we got to church I immediately felt a pain in my chest. The last time I was in church was the week before I graduated high school. As much as I went to church growing up, I was never extremely religious. Maybe it was the fact that I knew me and God couldn't see eye to eye about who I was supposed to love. Now I was bringing my female fiancé into a place that condemned what we had. I felt like we were going to melt the moment that we stepped foot in the door. I wanted to grab Ahvi's hand but I knew that would make it worse.

Stepping into the church was like going back in time. Nothing had changed in the eight years I'd been gone. The pews still looked like they were missing screws, the Bibles were still holding on for dear life, and they still had that ugly red carpet that I always hated. All those building fund offerings, where exactly did that money go to?

"Sister Willis. It's good to see you this morning." Pastor came from one of the back doors and hugged my mother tightly. It took me a minute to remember how he looked. He was this tall, slender man, with chocolate skin, and gray hairs peeking out of the side of his head and beard. I didn't know why I thought he was short and fat.

"Morgan, it's good to see you again after all these years." He gave me the same hug he gave my mama and then quickly turned to Ahvi. "And you must be?"

"This is Ahvi, Morgan's fiancé," my mother answered before Ahvi could open her mouth.

The pastor's eyes opened wide like he just saw a ghost. "Well, why don't we go back to my office to talk."

We followed him through the church to the back of the building. Seeing his office I finally realized where all the money went. It was almost as big as the sanctuary and, with the modern architecture, I could tell that it was recently remodeled. Preachers never ceased to amaze me.

When he entered his office, a small-framed woman sat in the corner with a tape recorder and a notepad on her lap. I didn't know how these consultations worked but it seemed a little odd to have her in the room.

"This is my secretary, Mavis. She's here to take notes because I like to be completely engaged with the couple."

I took a second look at the secretary and recognized where I knew her from. We competed in a pageant together when we were in junior high. She looked so different without the makeup and the big hair. I smiled at her and she returned the gesture.

"Now I usually just talk to the couple together and what they want during their ceremony, but since this is a different union, I think I just want to talk to Morgan first."

Ahvi and I both looked at each other with confusion. I was a little uncomfortable with what was going on and I didn't want Ahvi to leave the room. She obliged and walked out of the room to sit in his waiting area. I thought my mother would follow suit but when she sat down on the couch, I was a little thrown off.

"Morgan, I wanted to talk to you a little bit before we get into the ceremony aspect."

"Okay." I was so confused about where this was going.

"At what point do you think you strayed from the Lord?" He crossed his legs and folded his hands on his lap.

"Excuse me?" It took all I had to not jump off the couch and punch him in his eye.

"Well, with meeting your fiancé, I feel in my spirit and I'm sure your mother agrees that this whole homosexual relationship is just a cry for help."

I couldn't believe my mother. I understood she was still trying to deal with the fact that I was gay, but for them to turn this into a homosexual intervention was way out of line. I gave her a long glance, waiting for her to look at me. She kept her head down and shifted in her seat. I sat back in my seat and folded my arms.

"Why don't you just talk to me and maybe we can put you back on the path to righteousness."

I couldn't believe this was my life right now. Was this dude really going to try to pray me straight? If this was the game these people wanted to play, they were about to get coached.

"Pastor, I don't know what you and my mother are feeling in your spirit or what God is telling you, but this isn't a cry for help. I'm not with Ahvi to piss anybody off. This is not a fad I will grow out of. I love being with women."

The look I received from both him and my mama looked like I just said I slaughtered baby cows and buried the heads in the backyard. If shocking them was what it was going to take to get me and Ahvi back to London, never to return here again, then I was about to go out with a bang. I respected my mama and the church but I wasn't going to trade my happiness so that they could feel comfortable.

"Morgan, you do know what the Bible says about homosexuality?" He began to reach for his Bible and all I could do was roll my eyes.

"Of course she does," my mother chimed in.

"Do you know what the Bible says about judgment?" *I can play this game too, sir.* "Listen, I couldn't care less what anybody thinks about who I choose to spend the rest of my life with. I am going to be with her regardless and if you don't want to preside over the unofficial ceremony, than I will be more than happy to go back to Europe where several countries would be more than happy to marry us."

I gathered my stuff and got up from the couch. I wasn't going to stay in that room any longer and get bashed for being me. I was so over this whole thing and I had every intention of booking Ahvi and me tickets back home immediately.

I stormed out the room and Ahvi popped up out of her seat as soon as she saw me. I grabbed her arm and pulled her back through the church.

"What happened?" she asked as she trotted in her high heels behind me.

"We're going home."

"Without your mum?" I could hear the confusion in her voice as her breath began to become shallow. I stopped as soon as we reached the parking lot to explain what was going on.

"We're going to our home in London. I'm done dealing with these people."

"Excuse me." A small voice came from behind us. I turned to see Mavis. "I'm sorry to be nosey, but I couldn't help but to get involved."

I was so focused on making my point to my mother and the pastor that I completely forgot that she was in the room taking notes.

"We really appreciate it, Mavis, but it doesn't matter. Gay marriage isn't recognized in the state of Georgia anyway."

"True, but that doesn't mean you can't still have some sort of ceremony. I know your family may not be supportive, but since you're already here you might as well go through with your plans."

She handed me a piece of paper with a name and number on it.

"What's that?" Ahvi grabbed the paper out of my hand.

"That is my brother's information. He is a licensed officiate, he has a house big enough for a wedding, and he is very open-minded. Give him a call." She turned and proceeded back into the building.

"Hey." I tried to stop her in her tracks. "Why are you doing this?"

It took her a minute before she turned back around to face us. "Because everybody deserves to have their happiness." She walked back into the building.

I felt a smile cross my face. It was the first time that I looked at this town in a different light. I still wasn't sure if I was going to stay, but I was glad to know that there was an option here for us.

Chapter 25

Janette

Hurting Henry was not in my plans at all and it is way overdue for me to correct my mistake. The last thing I wanted was for him to hate me for the rest of my life. My pacing back and forth was beginning to burn a hole through my floor as I continued to figure out what I was going to do. I had to make sure he got his job back.

I stopped pacing and ran to my computer, which was sitting on my dining room table. I feverishly typed Don's name into Google, praying that something would come up. Don Perkins was a very popular name, but his general information happened to be on the first page of my search engine. None of this stuff was anything I could use to my advantage. It was only information about his businesses and where he was from. If I was going to help Henry, and ultimately myself, I needed something that was beneficial. I was beginning to feel my patience fading and I resorted to my last option. I grabbed my phone and dialed Millie's number. It was a stab in the dark, but it didn't hurt to try.

"Hey, girl, what's up," Millie answered on the second ring. It was almost like she waited by the phone to talk about people's business.

"Nothing, just doing some research. Let me ask you something. Do you know about a Don Perkins?" I didn't know why I was crossing my fingers, but I needed Millie to really be the *National Enquirer* right now.

"Don Perkins. Did we go to school with him?" It was almost like Millie was searching through her database in her brain.

"No, he is a businessman. He does a lot of stuff in Atlanta."

Millie got real quiet and I could actually hear her thinking over the phone. This could only mean two things: either she knew about him and had something really juicy, or she thought she heard the name before but had squat. I heard her whisper his name over and over again to herself, still searching for something.

"I know Trina used to date a Donald from Atlanta. I think he managed a lot of businesses."

As crazy as it sounds, that might actually lead to something. "Is Trina's number still the same?"

"Girl, you know that child ain't changed her number since the ninth grade."

Remember when I said there are benefits to having a best friend who knows everybody's business? This was definitely one of those benefits. She may not have had the tea, but she knew the person who did and that was just as good.

"Thanks, girl. I'll talk to you later." I tried to hang up the phone, when I heard Millie interject.

"Wait a minute. What's all the interest in Don Perkins? Is he a new project?"

Remember when I said there are also downfalls to having a best friend who is in everybody's business? The downfall was I was not exempt from "everybody." I loved Millie, but I didn't need her in this just yet.

"Naw, just need to handle some business with him." I knew that response would back her off me. She couldn't care less if it wasn't juicy.

"Okay, well what happened with you and Henry? Did anyone ever find him?"

I had quickly become over this conversation. I appreciated Millie giving me what I needed, but I was not in the mood to tell her anything about Henry and me.

"I'll talk to you later, Millie. Thanks for everything." I quickly hung up before she had a chance to interject again. I scrambled to find Trina's number and quickly dialed it.

Two hours of conversation with my homegirl gave me everything I needed to start putting my plan in motion. I got off the phone with Trina and retrieved the business card Don gave me the last time we had our little encounter. Looking back at it now, I should have just kept my mouth shut. I dialed his office in Atlanta and talked to his secretary.

"Yes, Mr. Perkins is in the office today. Would you like me to put you through?" She had such a sweet and naïve voice. *She must be trying to put herself through school or something.*

"Oh, no, thank you. I was just checking." I hung up the phone and quickly got dressed and made my way toward Atlanta.

The hour-and-a-half ride it took to get there seemed like it took me twenty minutes. If I was on a mission, there was nothing that was going to stand in my way. I walked into the building and searched which floor his office was on. I hopped on the elevator and headed up to the seventh floor. When I got off the elevator I fixed myself before I walked into his office. I peeked in the window to scope out the scene. I was fully prepared to outsmart the secretary, but it was just my luck I could see her doing the potty dance. I waited a few minutes and she darted right past me down the hall. I fixed my hair and made sure my boobs were up and in place before I stormed into Don's office.

"Can I help you?" Don asked as I sauntered to a chair
in front of his desk. He seemed a little uneasy, and I was
getting a little offended that he didn't remember me.

"I'm here to see you," I said in my sexy voice.

"Okay. Did you make an appointment with Christine?"

"Is that your teenager who sits at the desk outside?
Yeah, she wasn't at her post so . . ." I crossed my legs like
Sharon Stone in *Basic Instinct*. It took me a long time to
perfect this move and it worked every time.

"Have we met?"

I could see the wheels turning in his head, and I didn't
respond to his question. I just smirked seductively.

"The busy beauty from the deli," he finally blurted out.

"For a second there, Mr. Perkins, I thought you had
forgotten about me."

"I never forget beautiful women. So to what do I owe
this pleasant surprise? Are you here to thank me for
lunch?"

I thought it was cute that he felt like he had game just
because he had a little money. I was here to put a hole in
that balloon. I got up from my seat and walked around to
sit on his desk right in front of him. He needed to see all
of me because it was about to get serious.

"I am here to make you fix a wrong that we have both
committed."

His face went back to confusion. "Excuse me?"

"You have decided to terminate a deal you had pending
with Henry Lloyd and you are going to give him something better." I calmly straightened his tie as I talked.

"And why would I do that? You were right about that
business. It was dead from the gate." He sat back in his
chair as if he had one up on me.

I gave him a smirk and continued, "I'm a smart girl.
Though I was right about your little venture, that didn't
mean I wanted Henry to be out completely. I'm sure

with all your vast resources; you have a position for him somewhere." I tried to lean over a little so he could get a good look at my breasts. He leaned forward slowly and I figured I had him right where I wanted him.

"As thoroughly as I am enjoying this little act of yours, I've been successful for ten years and I'm not about to let some country tart flirt with me to get her boyfriend a job." He sat back in his seat and began to focus his attention back on his work. "You can go now."

If I didn't have ammo, I probably would have been offended. My daddy didn't raise no fool and I always had a backup plan.

"You're right. You shouldn't let a country tart tell you who to hire. I wonder if Daphne McKale may have something for Henry."

Don's eyes got big and I could see him trying to keep his composure. I loved this feeling: when I knew I had someone exactly where I wanted them and they never saw it coming.

"How do you know about Daphne?" he finally muttered.

I got up from his desk and began to walk around his office. I wanted to take my time and revel in this moment.

"How does it feel, Don? Concealing such a big secret for so long and then just like that some country tart walks in and pulls your pants down. No pun intended."

"I don't know what you want but—"

"On the contrary, you know exactly what I want. And I know exactly what you want." He stayed quiet so I continued, "I wonder what all your business partners will think if they find out you had an inappropriate affair with a sixteen-year-old girl and your mommy paid top dollar to make her go away and conceal it when she found out Daphne was keeping your baby."

I knew this was a low card to play, but I was going to do whatever it took to make sure Henry was set. I messed it up and I would fix it. I could see Don trying to choose his next move carefully.

"I was twenty-one years old."

"I'm sure that won't matter. Your whole claim to fame with your business partners is that you didn't need help from your judge father or heiress mother. I don't think they will be too happy that they are in business with a liar, not to mention a sex offender."

He remained quiet for a few seconds, still thinking. I could tell he was backed into a corner and any second now he was about to give me exactly what I asked for.

"What exactly do you want for Henry?"

I tried to conceal my victory smile. This plan worked beautifully. "Something equally as good as or better than the venture you were going to move forward with. Henry is smart, hardworking, and about the best deal closer you will ever find. You know if he works for you, he'll make you more money than one of your businesses."

I had no idea if any of this was true, but it sounded good coming out of my mouth and I was sure Henry would work his hardest to prove me right.

"I may have something in mind, but I have to make some phone calls first. If I have your word that you will forget you know anything about Daphne McKale, consider it done."

I loved when I completed a mission successfully. It gave me such a rush. I gave Don a smirk and headed toward the door.

"One last thing." I stopped right before I turned the handle to walk out. "When you tell Henry, I was never here." I didn't wait until he agreed; I just walked right out. I may not have been a lot of things, but I did get what

I wanted with the right amount of persuasion. I hoped I was able to redeem myself with Henry. I never wanted him to feel about me the way he felt that night at the bar.

Chapter 26

Henry

My head felt like I had three black college bands having a drum line competition in it. I woke up face down on my living room floor with a bucket next to me. The last time I felt like this I was in college. I managed to muster up enough energy to grab a glass of water and some Advil from the kitchen. I tried to remember how I got home, but all I kept seeing was Janette's face. I couldn't believe she was the one who sabotaged my deal with Don. I knew she was capable of some sneaky things but I could never imagine that she would mess with people's livelihood. I thought it was about time to leave all the women of the Maxson family alone.

I needed to figure out a way to get myself back to the place I was before Morgan ever showed up. I had to make sure Don got back on board with the plan and I needed to regain my player status. I couldn't believe I hadn't been with anybody since I heard Morgan was in town. Well, Janette, but she didn't count. I needed some guidance and I knew exactly who I needed to talk to to get it.

I needed to try to sober up before I go anywhere. I couldn't drive to see my mama with last night's disappointment all over me. I stumbled into the shower and finally got to a point where my body wasn't screaming for help. All the events of this past week swirled around in my head as the hot water ran across my body. I was ready to get Morgan completely out of my system and move on like she never existed. I straightened up enough to get dressed and make that drive out to the nursing home.

The two and a half hours it actually took me to get to the home seemed to be a distant memory when my mama was in front of me. She looked so beautiful and the nurse was telling me she'd been having several good days lately. I was so happy that she was doing well but I was a little upset with myself that I hadn't come to see her earlier. I was so consumed with my own problems that I forgot about my own mother.

"I heard you've been on your best behavior lately. You ain't been cursing the nurses out." I brushed her hair behind her ear with my hand like she liked it.

"They ain't been pissing me off this week." She gave the cutest chuckle, which made me smile. It was good to hear her talking like her old self.

"Mama, things have been hectic lately." I wanted to capitalize on her being in her right mind and get some sound advice while I still had the chance.

"What's the matter, baby?" She stroked my hand like she usually did when she was trying to make me comfortable enough to talk to her.

"It just seems like everything I had under control is slipping away from my fingers."

"Can't nothing slip away from you unless you loosen your grip. If you had it under control once, then you can get it back. It's just up to you." Listening to her was probably the best thing I had heard all week.

"I don't think that's all the way true, Ma. I think I lost Morgan forever."

"Did you ever really have her?" My mother's response was kind of shocking. The last time I was here she remembered Morgan and me being happy. She even said we belonged together. I wondered how clear her head was today.

"Ma, I thought you liked Morgan."

"I think she's lovely, but that girl didn't seem like she wanted to be tied down by no man."

I almost wanted to burst out laughing, as sad as the situation was. It was amazing that my mama could tell that Morgan didn't want to be with a man without even knowing it. Why was I so blind to it? "Well, you may be right about that, Ma."

We stared out of the window at the birds fighting over the food my mother had put out for them earlier. Birds were always my mama's favorite. She loved the different colors on them and how majestic it was to watch them fly. She had a special birdhouse for them when she was living at the house. She always had food for them and watched them during her breakfast. I thought they got so used to her, for the first few months after she moved they seemed like they were looking for her. It was sweet and sad at the same time. It made me miss her even more.

"Jimmy, you remember when we took that trip to DC? They seemed to have the best birds."

I had a sinking feeling in the pit of my stomach when I heard her say my father's name. "Ma?" I tried to touch her hand and look her in her eyes so that she could see me. She put her hand on my face and smiled.

"You were so handsome in your three-piece suit and I was getting so jealous of those girls staring at you."

I had such a mixed feeling of emotions with her statement. On one hand I thought it was a sweet thing that she was harping on the good times with my father; on the other hand I needed her to stay with me in the present. I wasn't ready for her to slip back.

"Ma, it's me, Henry. I'm your son." I needed her to come back to me, just for a little while longer. I tried to gaze deep in her eyes, hoping that she would come back. She gave me a smile and caressed my face and for a moment I thought that she actually saw me again.

"I love you, Jimmy. Don't ever leave me."

Tears began to roll down my face as I realized that she had left me. I was glad I got to have moments of clarity with her and I got what I came for, but I needed more time with her.

"I love you too," I said as I kissed her on her forehead.

I walked out the room to get some air. I didn't want to come apart in front of her. I didn't know how that would affect her and I wasn't trying to make anything worse. I paced up and down the hall, trying to pull myself together before I go back in her room. The ridiculous ring from my phone went off and it reminded me just how loud it actually was.

"Well, I'm glad to know you're alive," Beau said before I could even say hello. "Next time you decide to dip from a party, could you at least shoot a brotha a text or something?"

I swear he can be so extra sometimes. "My bad, dog. I just needed to get out of there." I'd learned that if you agreed with Beau and made your apology early, he'd move on from the subject faster.

"I feel you. So where you at now?"

See what I mean? He's on to a whole new subject.

"Visiting my mom. It's been a minute and I wanted to check in on her."

"Well, when you're done with that, I would suggest that you get back to the office ASAP. I ran into Don today and he's looking for you."

By the tone in Beau's voice it didn't sound like it was bad news. I didn't want to ask if he knew anything for fear of getting my hopes up. I hung up the phone with Beau and went to go spend a few more minutes with my mama. I was happy that it appeared that Don may not be done doing business with me, but I wanted to make sure that I didn't neglect the most important thing in my life. I spent so much time this week trying to get Morgan back, I could spend a few more moments with the woman who loved me unconditionally. Besides, she was right. Nothing would slip out of your fingers unless you loosened your grip. I had a plan on having a chokehold on things from now on.

Chapter 27

Janette

I had never felt so guilty about anything in my life as I did after Henry yelled at me in the bar. None of that was a part of my plan. I wanted him to see that I was the only one who had his back when everything fell, not the one who set up his demise. I didn't know why I had to open my big mouth. Maybe I didn't deserve him. Maybe that was my karma for all the resentment I had toward Morgan. It was just sad that now that Morgan was out of the picture, he didn't want anything to do with me. My father's funeral was only a day away and I needed to be focusing on my family.

My mother still didn't want to discuss what happened at the funeral home with my aunt Beanie, but at least she was out of her room. Everything was in place for Daddy's burial except we hadn't heard anything about his will. I was wondering what the process with that was and figured we should have at least heard from a lawyer by now. I wasn't sure if I should take care of it or if it was already handled by my mother but I wasn't prepared to ask. My mama and I sat in the kitchen, both playing with our food in silence. The house phone rang for the first time today and it kind of startled both of us.

"Answer that, Nettie. Whoever it is, I'm not here. I'm going back to bed." She got up from the table and walked back to her room.

I answered the phone as soon as she was out of my line of vision to make sure she wasn't involved in any lie I was about to tell.

"Good morning. This is Sonya Walker. I represented Mr. Joe Maxson with the changing of his will. Is Mrs. Maxson in?" the voice responded to my initial hello.

"Um, she's unavailable at the moment but this is his daughter Janette. Is there something I could help you with?" I thought it was ironic and kind of creepy that I was thinking about this very topic not even five minutes ago. I looked up at the ceiling as if I could see my dad staring down at me. I knew he was the one behind the timing of this.

"Well, I've been notified of the passing of your father and, upon his request, he would like his will to be read and executed before his burial."

"Well, we planned to have his funeral tomorrow." I felt like this was kind of sudden, but it was what my father wanted.

"Well, if there is an available time for you and your family to come in to my office today, I would be more than happy to make you an appointment."

I wasn't sure what my mother wanted to do, but it didn't sound like we had much time to do this. I set up the appointment with Ms. Walker and hung up the phone. I wasn't really concerned with my father's will because what he had, he had already put it into his family. Whatever he had left to give, I was sure it all went to my mother and the quicker we handled it, the quicker we could move on.

It felt like it took an act of God to get my mother to get out of the house and go to this meeting. I knew she was continuing to grieve, but it never stopped her from dealing with the business. One thing my mama was known for was making sure that the necessary things were taken care of regardless of the situation. It was extremely weird to see her not being herself.

When JJ, Mama, and I walked into Sonya's office, I was a little surprised to see Beanie and Uncle Earl already there. I knew they were close with my father, but I didn't know what my father had to give to Beanie that he already hadn't.

"Thank you so much for seeing me on such short notice," Sonya said as we took our seats.

My mama took a quick glance in Beanie's direction and then kept her eyes on the floor. It was really bothering me that there was something going on between those two and my mama wasn't telling me what it was.

"If we can just get this over with that would be great," I said, trying to speed up this intense process.

"I wish I could, but all parties have to be present before I can read any part of the will."

Now I was confused. What did she mean all parties have to be present? As far as I was concerned, everybody was here and then some.

"I'm pretty sure all parties are here. His immediate family is here and he wasn't really close to his brothers and sisters in order to leave them something in his will." I glanced over at Beanie who gave me a little sideways look. "Except for Aunt Juanita of course," I stated, trying to smooth things over. For the next two days, I was over the drama until my daddy was safe in the ground.

"Well, unless any of you are Morgan Willis, we have to wait."

Now I was really confused. What did Morgan have to do with anything? Morgan was just a niece and the last I heard, unless he set up a trust fund for his whole family, nieces really didn't get no play in the will. Was their bond

that strong to where he left her something in his will?
I looked around the room and noticed both my mom
and Aunt Beanie shifting in their seats. Something was
definitely up and I needed to know what was going on.

"I feel like you two know something that you aren't
sharing with the rest of us," I finally spoke up. Neither
one of them budged to say anything, which only pissed
me off.

"Why don't we just wait for Morgan and we can get this
all cleared up," Sonya interjected. "Does anybody know
when she will be coming?"

Aunt Beanie looked at her watch, then her phone
without a response. I knew my family had a lot of issues
but this was not like us.

"We're not sure if she's going to make it; she had
another engagement," my uncle Earl finally said.

Every second I stayed in this room without any action
was making me angrier. I didn't care if my daddy had
millions of dollars that we didn't know about and was
leaving it to a goat; I needed to know what my mama and
Beanie were hiding. Nobody was going to leave this room
until I get an answer.

"Well, legally, I can't proceed without her present."

"Something doesn't feel right and nobody is speaking.
Can somebody please tell me what's going on?" I didn't
realize that I was raising my voice until everyone was
looking at me like I had lost my mind.

"You might as well tell her, Beanie. He's dead now,
ain't no use in protecting him," my mother finally said,
which was the most I had heard from her in days.

"Protecting him from what?" I turned my focus on
Beanie since she seemed to be the one with all the
answers. The room grew silent and I could tell Beanie was
contemplating in her head what she should say next.

"We think Joe may have left Morgan some money," she
finally said.

I wanted to be angry but I wasn't even surprised. She and my father were close and it seemed like something he would do.

"Tell her why," my mother chimed back in.

"Is that really necessary right now?"

"He's dead, Juanita; might as well air out all his dirty laundry now. Isn't that what he wanted? As if he hasn't already caused enough drama."

I had never heard Mother raise her voice unless it was to discipline me or my brother. I knew this had to be serious if she had been taken out of her element.

Beanie took a long breath and began to explain what was going on.

"Joe is Morgan's father," she finally said.

I felt like I was having an out-of-body experience. It was like I had stepped out of my body and I was watching this from above. It was like I entered into a Shonda Rhimes episode.

"I'm sorry, what?" JJ asked before I could even get my thoughts together. I was glad I wasn't the only one in the room shocked by the news.

"A little before you were born, Nettie, Joe had an affair with this girl from Augusta—some girl who was a runaway from up North and had no family and no one taking care of her at the time. Joe didn't even know she was pregnant until she was almost eight months."

Every word Beanie was saying seemed to start sounding more and more like German. She really lost me around "Joe is Morgan's father." I honestly didn't know how much more messed up things could get. I glanced over at JJ and his reaction matched mine. It didn't seem like our brains were fully comprehending what was being told to us.

"She went into labor in a Walmart bathroom and died after giving birth. Joe was so afraid to come home and tell your mama that he had a child out of wedlock, so I agreed to take her in and raise her as my own. Earl and I had just lost a baby with no possibility of having any more children, so I felt like it was the right thing to do."

I didn't know how to respond to what I just heard. This couldn't be real life. *Tell me I am having a nightmare. Tell me that there are cameras everywhere and at any moment a director is going to yell "cut." Tell me anything but don't tell me this is real life . . . my life. Morgan is my sister?*

"Mama, did you know about this?" I finally asked.

"Only recently, when Juanita told me the story at the funeral home."

I couldn't believe what I was hearing. My father cheated on my mom and had a baby who my aunt raised as her own? Were they serious with this? And he wasn't man enough to tell us this while he was alive?

"I'm sorry," Beanie said as if she could read my mind.

I wanted to scream but my body seemed paralyzed. It couldn't move, I couldn't speak, I could barely comprehend what was happening. The only thing I could do was look over at my brother, who was in the same state of shock as I was. He couldn't believe what was going on either and for some reason that comforted me a little.

"You know what? Whatever is in that will he can keep. I don't want anything from him," I finally said.

I got up and stormed out of the office. I was so over this whole thing. It wasn't even the fact that Morgan was my sister; it was that we were completely lied to for my entire life. My dad didn't even have the balls to say it out loud to his own family. He had to reveal it to us in his will. He could keep whatever he wanted to give us to ease his conscience. I was done with everything.

Chapter 28

Morgan

The house that Mavis's brother, Michael, lived in was the most beautiful house I had ever seen. It wasn't even a house, it was a mansion. I didn't know what he did to make his money but I was very impressed with him thus far. We were escorted to the tea room for our meeting with him. When he walked in I was surprised that he was not something grander. He had a short frame and low-key demeanor, but looked exactly like Mavis.

"Hello, ladies. I'm sorry to keep you waiting," he said as he shook both of our hands and took a seat across from us.

"Your house is really beautiful," Ahvi said for the both of us.

"Well, thank you. It's a family home. So, Mavis tells me you ladies want a union ceremony."

I was surprised he wanted to get right to the point without any small talk, but I could appreciate him not asking all the uncomfortable questions. "Yes. I kind of agreed to get married out here without telling my parents that Ahvi was a woman. Then my pastor tried to pray it out of me like it's a disease. So now it's either this or go back home to London."

Michael stayed quiet but shook his head like he understood exactly where I was coming from. It was kind of odd and comforting at the same time. I wanted to say more, but it looked like he was thinking so I decided to remain quiet.

"And you were trying to do this when?" he finally asked.

"Tomorrow," both Ahvi and I answered together as if it would be less of a blow to him. I had never heard of anyone agreeing to do a wedding ceremony or union ceremony, as he called it, on such short notice. Mavis said he was open-minded; I hoped he could bust his mind wide open for this one.

"Wow, you two don't wait do you?" He gave a nervous chuckle, which made me chuckle nervously.

"If it's a problem we understand. We just didn't want to waste the tickets out here," Ahvi chimed in.

He went back to the thinking pose that he had before, which scared me a little now. I didn't know why I was really nervous about this, but all of a sudden I wanted to go through with a ceremony in Georgia. I hated that all the work my mama did would be done in vain.

"Ladies, you are catching me on such short notice, but I would love to officiate for your ceremony."

I let out an excited squeal that shocked me a little. The fact that there was somebody who had my back here gave me a sense of peace. I held Ahvi's hand a little tighter and sat there with a big smile on my face.

"Why don't I show you the grounds and we can go over the details."

Whatever excitement that I had quickly died once I started talking about the actual ceremony with Michael and his groundskeeper. I realized I had no idea who was coming, I didn't have all my floral arrangements handled, and I wasn't sure about the music or the food. My mother was the one who took care of all that and she wasn't really speaking to me at the moment. This was not the way

I wanted any of this to happen. I began to have a mini panic attack thinking about all the stuff that still needed to be done.

"Don't panic," Michael said, trying to rub my back. "I promise I will fill in the missing gaps and everything will be fine."

"Right; and if it's just you, me, Michael, and the ground-skeeper then we'll have a ceremony for just us," Ahvi reassured me.

I began to breathe normally and calm down. Maybe things would be okay. And Ahvi was right. If it was just the four of us, then it would be just the four of us. I didn't need anybody else but her. We built a life together and it wasn't based on who approved of it. Besides, I was still going to have my dream wedding in Spain like I had planned from the beginning.

We continued to walk through the house and the backyard, talking and planning. I held on to Ahvi the whole time thinking about our future together. It felt like things were looking up and I was praying this was the end of the drama.

Chapter 29

Henry

The whole ride back from the nursing home I was going over what I wanted to say to Don. I had a speech prepared if he was going to sever all ties with me and I had a speech prepared if he was ready to move forward. I was praying that the outcome was going to be the latter, but I wanted to make sure I was ready for both. I put all I had into my business and I was going to make sure that I took it to the highest possible level that I could. I had so much I wanted to do and things I wanted to take care of that I needed this opportunity to happen.

I pulled up on my lot and instantly felt butterflies in my stomach. I thought I was prepared, but I was the most nervous I had ever been in my life. I didn't know how much damage Janette did and I didn't want to go in there doing damage control on something that might not be able to be fixed. I walked into my office and Don was already sitting at my desk. Now I was even more nervous because I hoped I hadn't made him wait too long. There were so many thoughts going through my head, I was freaking myself out.

"Don, sorry to keep you waiting." I shook his hand with all the confidence I could muster up and took my seat behind my desk.

"Not a problem. I haven't been here long."

I exhaled slightly at those words. At least we were getting off to a good start. "So what brings you back down here?" I started just the way I had planned it in my head. "The last time we spoke, it sounded like you were a little uneasy about doing business with me."

"Understand that I respect you."

I smiled a little on the inside because my pops told me that respect was the greatest thing a man could earn. It was good to hear those words, especially coming from someone like Don Perkins.

"I do have to admit, I think we rushed the luxury rental idea without looking at it from all angles."

The little bit of hope that I had left in this venture was beginning to deplete. I was hoping that he came to say he was ready to move forward with it and he brought the contracts for me to sign on the dotted line. I began to gear up my rejection speech in my head.

"So I'm guessing you don't want to continue forward with that venture?" I asked to make sure we were on the same page.

"I don't think at this point it would be a good investment." There it was: the knife to my dreams. "However, there is another offer I would like to make you."

I perked back up. I could see the little glimpse of light still flickering on my hopes.

"My investors and I are starting this celebrity car race. It'll be twice a year; celebrities and well-established members of society will have to pay a retainer to enter, and they get to race their own car through a designated part of the country. I'm talking millions of dollars every race and we already have over thirty people signed up for it."

This sounded too good to be true. People paid money to race their own cars? How was that any better than what we were going into?

"I'm sorry, I'm not quite following you here. What exactly do you want me to do?"

"We want you to help organize the races. You would get to travel around the world, interact with the rich and famous, and receive a ten percent commission for every person who signs up to race."

I had never heard of anything like this before. I honestly thought it was a crazier idea than the luxury rental. I was stunned that Don was so passionate about it and not about the venture I brought him. It did sound appetizing, though. *It's an opportunity to get the hell out of Georgia, and I may be making some real big money.*

"Okay, so you have almost thirty people ready to sign up? How much is the entry fee?" I needed to know how much 10 percent was going to be for me.

"A quarter million," he said so nonchalantly.

"Wait a minute. You're telling me that people have to pay $250,000 to enter this race?" I asked in amazement.

"That's correct."

"And twenty-five thousand of that would be mine?" I was still amazed.

"That's correct."

"And there are already thirty people who are willing to put up the money right now." I was hoping he would say those two beautiful words again.

"That's correct."

I swore I could have kissed this man right now. I was so excited about this opportunity. It was different and a little unbelievable but it seemed solid. My main concern with all of this was what would happen to my business and what would happen to my mama. I wouldn't want anything to happen to her while I was traveling for business and I couldn't get to her fast enough. $25,000 a person though was definitely enough to get her out of that nursing home and into some top-notch home care.

"Look, you don't have to say yes today. Think about it, sleep on it, but I need an answer soon. We are trying to get the ball rolling on this thing immediately."

He stood up, buttoned his coat jacket, and extended his hand toward me. I saw my whole future in this man. Everything I wanted to be, everything I had worked so hard for to get me to this point was right there in front of me. I could hear my pops now saying I would be a fool to pass this opportunity up.

"Mr. Perkins," I said as I grabbed his hand, "count me in."

"Good man." He chuckled and made his way to the door. "I'll send you over all the information and paperwork. See you soon, partner."

He walked out and as soon as the door closed behind him I burst out into the touchdown dance I used to do. I couldn't be more excited. My mother was right. Nothing slipped out your fingers unless you loosened your grip. My life was about to change and I was so ready for it. I plopped down in my chair and took a deep breath. I felt like I had made it, and with all the mess I placed myself in recently, I wasn't planning on looking back.

Chapter 30

Janette

What had my life amounted to? No man; a lying, dead father; and a cousin who was really my half-sister. I used to get offended about people saying how country folks in Georgia were, but this was for real some country mess. I couldn't even fathom how sneaky my father had to be in order to pull this off for so many years. I hated that I was so much like him. All the manipulative stuff I'd done over the years flashed before my eyes the more I dwelled on my father's infidelity.

My bed seemed to be my safe haven over the last week and a half. It was where I retreated to whenever things were getting too much and today was no different. I didn't move from the fetal position from the time I left the lawyer's office and crawled in here. I hadn't even seen my apartment in several days. I thought it would be awkward to stay at my parents' house after what we just found out but I wanted to be close to my mom.

"You okay?" my brother said as he got in the bed next to me and held me tight.

"What do you think?"

"I think you're feeling the same way I am."

"Angry that our father was a liar and a coward?" I could feel JJ shake from trying to chuckle silently.

"I was going to say shocked and confused, but I guess angry is an accurate emotion to have."

It amazed me how levelheaded JJ could be through all this. He was definitely more like Mama than I was.

"I just don't get it, J. How could he do that to us? To Mom?"

"Who knows what they were going through at the time?" There was the levelheadedness again. I couldn't understand how he remained so calm about the situation. I was steaming from my eyeballs. I was so mad I couldn't even cry if I tried.

"Yeah, but to lie to your wife and children for twenty-six years is beyond me. I mean, am I even mom's child or did he have another mistress?"

My brother laughed out loud this time. "Trust me, you definitely belong to Mom. I remember when she was pregnant with you and all I wanted to do was poke her belly with a stick."

We both laughed at his comment. I wished I would have known my brother was trying to play human piñata with our mother. I appreciated my brother's humor but I was still very angry.

"I don't think I want to go to the funeral tomorrow."

My brother sat up in the bed and turned me toward him. He scanned my face for a moment to make sure that I knew what I was saying. "Are you serious?" he finally asked.

"Yes. I don't know if I can handle it. I have lost all respect for that man and I can't go to a thing where people are glorifying him."

The look in my brother's eyes was one of hurt. I couldn't tell if it was from the situation or from the comment I just made. Either way, it kind of made me sad to look at.

"Look, I know you are hurt but that is our father. You have to go tomorrow."

"How can I look those people in the face and be sincere? How am I supposed to look Morgan in the face and not see twenty-six years of lies?"

My brother took a moment before he spoke. He glanced around the room almost like he was searching on my dressers for the words to say next. "Don't take this out on Morgan. Cousin, sister, whatever, she has always been family. And she is an innocent bystander just like us."

"He had a special relationship with her because he knew all along. Do you know I hated her for that? I felt like he was closer to her than he was to me and it was because he knew he made a mistake that he couldn't fix." I felt the tears creeping up. My anger began to turn into hurt as I continued to talk about my father. I thought I was past the crying, but knowing the reason why my dad was the way he was with Morgan brought back all those old feelings of resentment.

"He made a horrible mistake." My brother began to wipe my tears from my cheek. "And you . . . we have every right to be mad at him. But tomorrow we need to recognize him for all the good that he was. Because if you don't say your last good-bye to Dad before they put him in the ground, I promise you'll be angrier with yourself than you would ever be at him."

JJ kissed me on my forehead and hopped off my bed. He picked up the picture of my father and me when I was a little girl that I had knocked down in anger and placed in on my bedside table.

"Get some rest, we got a big day tomorrow." He walked out the room and shut my door behind him. He always did that when he felt like I needed to be alone with my thoughts.

I loved and hated my brother for being so understanding. I wanted to be angry. I wanted to be justified in my emotions and here he came making me feel bad.

I glanced over at the picture of us. I remembered that day like it was yesterday. It was the first time he ever took me to the county fair. I was around eight and I was just big enough to ride all the rides. I was so excited that it was just me and Dad because JJ got in trouble at school and couldn't go. He let me eat as much food and candy I wanted and rode every single ride with me until I threw up everything I ate. It was literally the best day of my life.

Tears began to fall down my face as I thought about the moments when he was the greatest dad in the world. I was so blinded by my jealousy about his and Morgan's relationship, I didn't recognize the one I had with him. JJ was right. If I didn't say my last good-byes tomorrow, I would regret it for the rest of my life.

I closed my eyes and prayed that the Lord work on my heart and give me the strength for forgiveness. I was going to need a lot of that in the morning.

Chapter 31

Morgan

I didn't think I had ever felt weirder in my life than I did waking up this morning. I wasn't prepared to go to my uncle's funeral today and I was even less prepared for my union ceremony right after. I had absolutely no idea how Michael pulled together the loose ends to our ceremony but he told me everything was taken care of. I still wasn't sure who was coming but I informed everyone about the change in location. Whoever showed would be welcomed, and whoever didn't would not be missed.

I showered and dressed quickly for the funeral. I had butterflies the whole time almost to the point of throwing up. The faster this day was over with, the faster I could get back to normal life. All this commotion was giving me heart palpitations.

I walked into the kitchen and it appeared I wasn't the only one who got dressed early. They all sat solemn at the table, trying to keep down the little bites of food they were putting in their mouths. I couldn't understand how they could eat. My stomach was doing back flips, cartwheels, and summersaults. I would be happy if I could make it through the day without having to go to the bathroom every ten minutes. I wanted to speak, but the vibe was so intense that it felt like I was walking on landmines. Any sudden movement and the whole thing would go up in smoke. Everyone was being cooperative and I was going to keep it that way; at least for today.

"We better get a move on if we're gonna make the procession in time," my father said as he got up from the table, taking sips of his last little bit of coffee.

The plan was that everyone was going to meet at Uncle Bug's house and ride the procession from there. I could only remember being in one of these things when my grandma died and I just remembered a lot of cars. We gathered our stuff and proceeded to our meeting spot.

When we arrived at Uncle Bug's house it was pure chaos. Being a part of nine siblings meant that there was a lot of immediate family. Cousins, aunts, and uncles I hadn't seen in years were all at the house. Some people noticed that I had Ahvi on my arm and inquired about her, some people were so distraught they didn't even notice, and some people just stared. It was a little uncomfortable, but this moment wasn't about Ahvi and me; it was about Uncle Bug and I was going to make sure it stayed that way.

We weren't at the house long before the funeral director instructed us to proceed to our assigned cars. I finally saw JJ and Janette when I was making my way to the third limo, but there was too much going on for me to speak to them. I hoped that there would be sometime today when I could clear the air, especially with Janette. I knew her emotions were pretty high right now, but I wanted her to know that I had nothing against her. We're family and I wanted us to have a mutual love and respect for each other.

The car ride to the church was really sad. It began to hit me that my favorite uncle was no longer here. I wasn't going to be able to call him long distance and joke about random things. Tears began to fall and I was thanking God for waterproof mascara because I would be a train wreck for our ceremony later. I sat next to my mom on the ride there and she grabbed my hand once she realized

I was crying. It made the tears fall down more because it was the first loving interaction we'd had in a few days.

"Baby, I want you to know that no matter what, I have always and will always love you." She lifted up my head and it was the first time me made solid eye contact since Ahvi arrived.

"I know, Mama." I lifted her hand to my mouth and kissed the back of it.

"Before we go in I need to tell you something."

The car stopped and I looked out the window to see that we'd arrived at the church. The funeral director navigated all the cars behind the limos into the parking lot and opened the doors of the vehicles that we were in, motioning us to get out and line up.

"How 'bout we talk afterward, okay?" I kissed my mama on the cheek and got out of the car.

It took us at least twenty minutes to get lined up and ready to walk in the church. Ahvi rode with me in the limo but didn't think it was appropriate to walk in with me. I made sure she got in the church and to a decent seat before I lined up with the rest of my family. When we began to walk I took a deep breath and tried to keep my composure.

Walking down the aisle of the church toward my uncle's body was so overwhelming. I could hear people wailing and it made me even more emotional. This was the first time I'd seen my uncle since he died and I wasn't sure I could handle it. When I saw my mama almost pass out and my dad have to carry her to her seat, I was a little over my head. I broke down as soon as I saw him. Beau quickly moved next to me and grabbed me before I passed out like my mom. He helped me to my seat and I was so grateful that he was there.

The pastor started the service as soon as the last family member sat down. I really wasn't paying attention but it sounded like it was the normal hoopla that they say at a funeral. It wasn't until he started reading the eulogy that was printed in the program that I actually started listening.

"He is survived by his wife and two children," he read aloud.

"Three."

At first I didn't know who blurted that out, but then I saw people looking toward Janette. She stood up and JJ tried his best to sit her back down. "I just want to make sure that there are no lies in his eulogy. He is survived by his three children."

I had no clue what had gotten into Janette, but it was not the time or place. Everyone around her was trying to tell her to sit down and not make a scene, but she looked determined to get whatever was bothering her off her chest. If this weren't a funeral it may have been entertaining, but it was just sad and inappropriate.

"I mean, my father had been lying for over twenty-five years, so why not tell the truth when he's dead? He has three children. JJ, me, and Morgan."

The gasps around the church were out of control. It was almost like she said "Morgan," but I know that couldn't be me. There was no way that was possible.

"What is she talking about?" I turned to my parents and they had looks of shock and guilt on their face.

"That's what I wanted to talk to you about."

I was so confused about what was going on and why it was going on now.

"In case you didn't know, you are our half sister, not our cousin, the product of Joe Maxson and a runaway who died having you." The words coming out of Janette's mouth were so unbelievable, which was why I didn't understand why it hurt so bad hearing them.

I looked at my parents once again and the looks on their faces told me everything I needed to know. I looked around the church and realized all eyes were on me. The only reaction I could do was to get up and get out of there as fast as I could.

"Morgan." I heard both of my parents call after me, trying to get me to stay. I ran out into the parking lot and began to weep uncontrollably. What the hell was going on?

"Morgan." My mom and dad—or aunt and uncle—came right out behind me.

"What the hell was she talking about?" I immediately needed answers. I didn't want to hear their excuses. "Is Bug my father?"

"Yes," my mother blurted out. I almost dropped to my knees. "Joe had an affair and your birth mother died in labor, so we took you in as our own. But, Morgan, you are ours. We raised you, we loved you, and we will always consider you our daughter."

I tried to catch my breath but this was making my head spin. "You guys lied to me," I finally said.

"We were trying to protect you." My father interjected this time. "You were still blood and we gave you a good home."

What they were saying right now was irrelevant. I was so hurt. "You two keep something so huge from me, but you have the audacity to be upset about hiding the person I'm in love with from you. I should have never come back."

"Morgan, please don't hate us. We were only trying to do what's right." My mother tried to walk toward me but I backed up. I wasn't in the mood for her comfort.

"What's in the lockbox under your bed?" I knew it was an odd question, but I needed to know if it was connected.

"What?" My mother's fake confusion face wasn't fooling anybody.

"The lockbox under your bed. What's in it?" I had never raised my voice to my parents before, but seeing as these weren't my real parents I didn't feel as bad right now.

"They're your birth records and official adoption papers."

My whole body was numb. I knew I wasn't going crazy. I couldn't be around these people one more minute. I needed to get out of here like now. I turned and began to trot down the road in my heels. I had no idea where I was going but anywhere was better than being in a room with my so-called family. My whole world has been turned upside down and I really didn't know what I was going to do. All I wanted to do was just go back to London where I belonged.

Chapter 32

Henry

I couldn't believe Janette would make this huge scene at her dad's funeral. I'd seen some messed-up black funerals but that one definitely topped anything I'd ever seen. Everyone in the church was afraid to make a move after the bomb Janette dropped exploded. I felt extremely bad for Morgan. I couldn't imagine what she was going through right now. The pastor put a rush to the service and we were out of there in less than thirty minutes. Any longer than that and it would have been unbearable to be there.

When it was over I didn't make my way to the grave-yard like everyone else. I had to go find Morgan. I felt like I was the only one who would be able to find her and talk her off the ledge. After driving around for fifteen minutes I ended up by the creek, where I spotted her throwing rocks into the water. I got out the car and made my way toward her. I picked up a rock and skipped it alongside of her.

"You were always good at that," she said through tear-soaked eyes.

"I had to have some sort of skill to fall back on in this world. You see how football turned out for me." She laughed and I was happy that I could still bring her a little comfort.

"I'm so screwed up, Henry." She fell on the ground and put her face in her hands and began to cry.

It broke my heart to see her like this. We may have had our issues but I still cared about her. I sat down next to her and pulled her in my arms. "I don't think you're screwed up. I think you are a product of some very unfortunate events and finding out about it is hard."

She lifted her head from my chest and wiped her face. "I found out that my dead uncle is really my father and my parents adopted me to cover up his affair. I think I am screwed up."

"Okay, so it is a pretty bad situation, but at the end of the day they are still your blood relatives. Think about it. Even though your uncle didn't step up as your dad, he was still in your life. And he made sure you had a good home. He could've not cared what happened to you or your birth mother." I surprised myself by how profound I sounded.

"You're right, but I still think they should have told me at some point."

"Maybe they should have but the end result is that you know now. And, yes, Janette was a complete jerk for doing it that way, but I'm pretty sure she's hurt too." I didn't know why I just defended Janette when she tried to ruin my life too, but I was trying to move past that.

"How did you know I was here?" Her voice indicated that she was slowly but surely coming out of the self-pity.

"We grew up together, remember? I know you just as well as you know me."

"I was such a jerk to you the other day. I'm really sorry about that." She laid her head on my shoulder and it made me smile a little.

"Yes, you were." I chuckled. "But it's cool, you were being honest. And I think we both agree that is something people around here need to do more often."

She laughed hysterically and I couldn't help but to laugh too. This had been the most stressful week for all of us and at this point it seemed like the only thing left to do was laugh.

"You want to hear some amazing news?"

"Uh, yeah. That's like asking a homeless guy if he wants a warm place to sleep." Her humor was getting dark. I kind of liked it but it scared me a little.

"I'm giving the business to Beau and I'm going to travel around the world for a multimillion dollar company."

Her mouth dropped when she heard and she wrapped her arms around me. "Henry, that's amazing. Congratulations."

"Thank you. I'm really excited about it. I leave in two weeks, New York is my first stop." It was almost surreal saying it out loud. I had never imagined myself being in this place, but I was happy about it.

"Wow, that's really great. You'll love New York, but do you really trust Beau with the business?"

"Not really, but he deserves it." It was good talking to Morgan like this without arguing about the past. I could be comfortable with being just friends with her. The sun was beginning to beat down on us and I figured that I had done all I could to cheer her up; and now it was time to get her show on the road.

"Okay, so the way I see it we could continue to sit here and feel sorry for ourselves, or I could get you somewhere to get ready for your ceremony. Because the last time I checked there is a very fine European woman walking around here wanting to marry you."

"Oh my God, Ahvi. I completely forgot. Can you give me a lift to Brookwood Manor?" She hopped up off the ground and stuck her hand out to pull me up.

I grabbed her hand and pulled myself up from the ground. I gazed in her eyes and I didn't see a past lover, or a girl who broke my heart. I saw someone who I cared about and would always have as a friend.

"I would be honored." I stuck out my arm for her to hook hers inside of it and escorted her to the car. "How did you get down here anyways?" I asked as we began to walk toward my car.

"I stole some random kid's bike."

We both laughed and I was completely at peace with the relationship I was beginning to build with her.

Chapter 33

Janette

Everyone was still up in arms about my outburst in the church, but I felt like it was the right thing to do. Everyone had been lying for so long I just wanted it to stop. It may have not been the most appropriate way to do it but it was definitely necessary. My mother and brother were completely pissed off at me after the service.

"I cannot believe that you not only embarrassed yourself, you embarrassed the whole family, your father, and Morgan," my mother fussed as we rode to the graveyard.

"What were you thinking, Nettie?" JJ added. "I thought you were going to chill."

"I thought I was too, but I couldn't hold it in. She deserved to know." I felt justified in my actions and I wasn't going to have them guilt me out of that.

"She did, but not like that." The disappointed look that my brother gave me completely crushed my soul. I hated that look. When we got to the graveyard I decided not to get out. I thought I showed out enough; I didn't want to cause any more drama.

I watched my mom and JJ walk through the graveyard holding each other and grieving. I wished I could put my anger aside and just honor my father like I was supposed to, but I couldn't trust myself to behave. When the car door opened I immediately jumped. Beau climbed in and stared at me with his own disappointed look.

"What now?"

"You know what you did was messed up, right?" he said like it was a brand-new proclamation.

"You aren't the first one who's told me that, Beau."

"Look, I don't know what you've had against Morgan all these years, but that's family. Whether you like it or not you can't trade her, so you might as well accept it."

The words weren't anything I hadn't heard before, but coming from Beau it felt different. He was usually the fool, not the voice of reason.

"So what do you think I should do?" I hated asking that question to anybody but I needed to try a slice of humble pie right now.

"Well, an apology is a good place to start." And just like that he jumped out the car and headed toward the burial site.

I hated the fact that everyone was right and they were making sense. I had been a little brat toward Morgan over the years for no reason. I had a sister this whole time and I never treated her the way she deserved to be treated. Beau and JJ were right. We were family and I couldn't change that if I tried. I decided that it was time to put away my insecurities and make it right with Morgan. She was my sister after all.

After the burial, everyone had to rush to get changed and head to Brookwood Manor. It was the first gay union ceremony I thought any of us had ever attended, so I was sure it would forever be the talk of the town, true Morgan style.

Walking into the manor was like crossing over into a different world. I had never seen something so beautiful in my life. If I weren't here to make amends, my jealousy would have gotten the best of me. I had no idea how they pulled this off so quickly, but everything looked amazing. I walked around to try to find out where Morgan would be getting ready. I climbed up this grand, winding staircase and listened out for talking. I heard giggling from a room at the end of the hall and followed the noise. I poked my head in to see if it was her, and I saw her and who I presumed to be her fiancé helping each other get ready.

"Isn't it bad luck to see the bride before the ceremony?" I said from the doorway. I was ready for Morgan to give dagger eyes but instead she could barely look at me.

"I think we can manage the bad luck," the fiancé said. "You must be Janette. I'm Ahvi." She walked toward me and gave me a hug and kiss on the cheek. "I'll let you two talk." She walked out the room and closed the door.

I had to admit that Morgan looked stunning in her dress. She was absolutely a breathtaking bride.

"I know you may not want to talk to me, but I just wanted to say I'm sorry. The way I behaved today—hell, the way I've behaved our whole lives—was unfair and misdirected."

She walked toward me without saying a word and pulled me into her arms.

My whole body was numb. I had no idea what was going on or what to do next. I didn't know if this was a trap or what.

"I forgive you," she whispered in my ear.

I pulled away to look at her face. Was she serious? It was that easy? *I just admit that I'm wrong and, poof, I'm forgiven?*

"Are you serious right now?" I asked in confusion.

"Look, this week and a half was awful. But it taught me that family, no matter how dysfunctional, is important. I haven't been the greatest cousin or sister or whatever."

"Yeah, but you didn't deserve the way I treated you."

"Maybe not, but it's in the past. Right now, today, at this very moment, I would love your support as I walk out there and commit to the woman of my dreams."

I smiled and hugged her this time. I didn't know what the future would bring but I was happy to oblige her wishes right now in the present. I pulled her veil over her face and escorted her out the room. My family had a lot of issues, but it was never boring; especially when you crammed a whirlwind of events all in one day.

Chapter 34

Morgan

I was surprised that Janette decided to bury the hatchet with me, especially with that whole fiasco at the funeral. I hadn't been prepared to forgive her so quickly, but I was tired of the drama and today was my wedding day. I was about to marry the love of my life. Ahvi was everything I wanted in a partner, and I was so honored that she felt the same about me. It was a huge release that I could move past this family drama and get back to being blissfully happy.

Janette and I walked out the bedroom I was getting ready in and the butterflies hit before I could walk down the stairs. I grabbed Janette's arm and stopped her in her tracks.

"You okay?" She put her hand over mine and stroked it.

"I'm not sure if I can do this." I tried to catch my breath and calm my heart rate.

"What? Marry this woman or walk down these stairs without falling? 'Cause the cat's out the bag about you being a lesbian."

I gave her a little chuckle. The truth was definitely out in the open and I didn't regret it at all. It's just the way I left things with my parents had me uneasy. I didn't want what happened in the parking lot of the church to be the last interaction I had with them before I walked down the aisle. Regardless of what transpired over recent events, I felt like I needed my parents here.

"I don't know if I can do this without my parents."
Janette dropped her head and I could tell that she felt bad for being partly responsible for how things went down a few hours ago. I could see her searching for something to say to ease my conscience.

"I know our family had some messed-up secrets, but Beanie and Earl love you."

"I know. I just would have liked if they could accept me and be here for support." I was trying to hold back the tears I felt welling up in my eyes.

"Ask and you shall receive," she said, and nodded her head toward the bottom of the stairs to direct my eyes at my parents.

We carefully continued down the stairs and I stopped directly in front of the people I knew as my parents. It was still unbelievable to me that they were biologically my aunt and uncle.

"I'll leave y'all to talk." Janette slipped her arm from under mine and walked out toward the ceremony space.

I was standing in front of my parents, holding my breath, and praying that this encounter would be a lot better than the last one we had.

"You look absolutely beautiful, baby girl." My father spoke up first with a tear in his eye.

"Thank you, Daddy, or Uncle Earl. I don't know which one I should call you now." I wasn't trying to be disrespectful. I really had no clue what was what anymore.

"I will always be your daddy," he said kind of matter-of-factly.

"We're sorry we didn't tell you sooner. I made a promise to Joe right after we took you in that I wouldn't say anything until he was dead and gone, and when it happened I couldn't bring myself to say the words."

My mother's speech was endearing and I could hear all the regret she carried in her voice. I couldn't find the words to respond so I let her continue.

"Junebug loved me enough to give me something that I could no longer give to myself. And he loved you enough to give you the home you deserved. You see, baby girl, God doesn't make mistakes. You and I were meant to be." My mother's words were tugging at my heartstrings, and the fact that tears were flowing down her face didn't make it any better.

I was trying my hardest for the sake of my makeup but I could no longer hold it in. I burst into tears and leapt into my mother's arms. She was right. I was fortunate to have the parents I did with the childhood they gave. I didn't always like my childhood, but it probably would have been much different if Bug hadn't cared so much.

"I love you, Mama," I whispered in my mother's ear.

"I love you too, baby."

I finally lifted up from her embrace. She wiped the tears from my face and fixed my makeup. I gave her a genuine smile from my heart and realized that I loved her even more for what she did for me and her brother.

"Now that that's done, you sure you want to go through with this ceremony?" my daddy interjected.

I took a deep breath and prepared myself to go back into this homosexual battle.

"Guys, I know that this isn't the ideal marriage that you had been dreaming about my whole life, but Ahvi is the most interesting, kind, loving, respectful person I have ever met. She loves me unconditionally and, at the end of the day, isn't that what you want for me?"

My parents looked at each other, waiting for someone to speak up first. I dropped my head in disappointment because I just knew they were about to turn and walk right out of here.

"Well, I guess I better get you down that aisle then." My father stretched his arm out for me to hook on to and my face lit up. I grabbed hold of his arm and tried to stop the tears from flowing once again. I didn't need my face to go through any more trauma before I saw Ahvi.

My father guided me toward the ceremony space, while my mother skipped ahead to take her seat. We walked out where I could see everyone seated. I wasn't expecting to see anyone here, but my whole family came out. Some people were still in their black outfits from Uncle Bug's funeral. Those people were only here for the spectacle of seeing two women go at it. If I weren't so anxious to get this over with I would have had them removed, but my focus was strictly on Ahvi.

Everything looked so beautiful. I had no idea where they were able to get all these purple orchids from on such short notice, but they adorned the rows and bridal arch that was at the end of the aisle. I was extremely excited to see the Plexiglas runner that flared out into a mini stage at the end. I was not about to walk and stand on that grass and have my heels sink into the dirt. The music started playing and I knew that was my cue.

"This is it, kiddo. You ready?" I could feel my father shaking.

"Absolutely." I slapped a smile on my face and took a deep breath. My moment was finally here.

Walking down the aisle almost felt like walking on stage at a pageant, except I actually wanted to be here. I could hear a couple of gasps and ahs as my father and I walked slowly down the aisle. I wanted to look around to see the faces that came but my eyes were fixated on Ahvi. She looked so amazing. A white body-hugging dress with lace and beading detail adorned her tall, slender frame. Her makeup was simple with a splash of color on her lips, and her hair was in an elegant bun. I had seen Ahvi look great before, but I had never seen her look more beautiful than she was right now standing at the end of the aisle.

My father and I ended what seemed like a twenty-minute stroll and a tear fell down Ahvi's face when we were eye to eye. My father stuck out his hand and softly grabbed Ahvi by the fingertips.

"We didn't get much time to get to know each other, but I'm entrusting you with my most precious gift. Please be good to my baby," he said just loud enough for the three of us and the official to hear.

"Believe me, I wouldn't dream of being anything but."

My father placed Ahvi's hand in mine and took his seat next to my mother. I looked into Ahvi's eyes and saw our beautiful past and our hopeful future. She gave me so much strength and love over this last year and especially this weekend. I was put at ease with having my family know the real me and them witnessing me marrying this amazing woman. The official started his speech and I floated through the ceremony as if I were on a cloud. This was what pure bliss felt like. I guessed my mother's favorite statement was the theme song to my life. *God doesn't make mistakes. Well played, Lord.*

Chapter 35

Henry

I had to admit, for my first lesbian commitment ceremony, I enjoyed myself. Both of the brides looked gorgeous from head to toe. I wanted to say that it was really sad that two women this fine ain't trying to mess with the male species, but listening to Morgan's vows I could tell she was really in love. It was definitely not the same for her and me. I had never seen that look in her eyes when she looked at me or heard her talk so passionately. I couldn't hate on that. It put me more at peace with us moving on as just friends, and I was happy that she was happy.

The ceremony only took about forty-five minutes and now everyone had begun to party at this reception/reunion banquet. It was amazing how these people could just hop from one event to another, but I guessed that's what family did. I was just happy that we didn't have to move to another location and there was an open bar. I spotted Beau at a table macking his cousin's sorority sister. I made my way over to him to mess up his game.

"There you are, you big chocolate man," I said, trying my best to sound like a gay man.

"Man, get outta here with that." Beau did not seem impressed with my antics.

"Oh, so now you don't know me after all the years we have together? Is he telling you he's different from any man you'll ever meet? I wonder why, girl."

Both the girl's and Beau's faces were absolutely price-less, and it was taking all I had not to burst out in laughter. Beau seemed to be irritated and I was loving every minute of it. It was very rare that I got to throw salt in Beau's game, so I made the best out of it.

"I didn't know you two were together. I'm really not trying to be in the middle of this." She got up and tried to walk away.

Beau grabbed her hand to try to plead his case. "Baby, he's just playing. We're just friends."

"Yeah, right. I know all about you down-low brothas. You don't fool me."

I waited until she walked out of ear range before I started to hysterically laugh in Beau's face. He wasn't amused, but tears were beginning to roll down my face and I was having a hard time catching my breath.

"Not cool, bruh. She was fine." He grabbed his glass and took a big gulp while I tried to catch my breath.

"Yes, she was," I tried to say through gasps.

"What the hell you come over here messing up my flow for anyway?" He took a sip of his drink, still a little upset that I messed up his game.

I wiped the tears from my eyes and tried to slow my heart rate. All jokes aside I did need to talk to him about important business. I never thought I would be telling my best friend that I'd be leaving without him for a better opportunity, because we were supposed to ride together, but I had to. Besides, even if I could take Beau along, I doubted he would ever truly leave home.

"I wanted to talk to you about the business."

"Man, if this is about me takin' the Escalade out the other night, my bad, bruh; but Vanessa was too fine to be rollin' in my car."

I could feel myself about to react, but at this point it didn't matter because he was about to become the boss. "Because I have big news for you, I won't even get into that. Beau, I think it's time for you to take over the company."

Beau's face had a mixture of confusion and excitement on it. I could tell he was searching for a proper response. "Wait, if I'm taking over what will you be doing?"

"I'll still be an owner, but I've gotten an opportunity to travel for a different company and I'm going to take it."

I had been so excited about my new position, but saying it out loud now to Beau it was a little sad. It was becoming real that I was about to leave everything that I knew behind.

"You're leaving and you're going to let me run your baby for you?"

"Yeah. You are like my brother and I trust you one hundred percent."

Beau's silence was kind of worrying me. I had no idea what he was thinking. I needed him to want this because it would be hard for me to leave unsure of the state of my company.

He took another sip of his drink and then stood from his chair. "Bruh, I'll be more than happy to take over for you." He extended his hand toward me.

A big smile spread across my face, and I grabbed his hand and stood to give him a hug. I knew I would be able to count on him. Beau may have had his issues but he was as dependable as they came.

"This means I get to have whatever car I want and give myself a salary right?" he asked in my ear as we continued to hold our embrace.

Maybe I spoke too soon on him being able to handle being in charge. I pushed him off of me and gave him a look that said, "Don't play about my money."

"I'm just playin', man." He chuckled. "I'm happy for you. Go out into the world and do great things. You know I'll hold you down here."

I loved that things looked to have a happy ending. Morgan and I were friends and I got to see her marry the love of her life; I was about to embark on an opportunity of a lifetime; and Beau was going to flourish as a businessman. It was like I had made the winning touchdown at the Super Bowl, so I didn't understand why I wasn't completely at peace. I looked past Beau's shoulder to see Janette sitting by herself, nursing a drink. I told Beau I'd catch up with him a little later, and made my way over to her. A piece of me still wanted to be mad at her for almost ruining my life, but with the way things turned out it was only right for me to let it go. *If I can be friends with my lesbian ex-girlfriend, I think I can make amends with her sister.*

"Not having a good time?" I took a seat beside her and crossed my hands on the table. She didn't make eye contact with me, and watched as Morgan laughed and danced with Ahvi.

"I think people are keeping their distance after what happened at Daddy's funeral." She gave a saddened smirk and took a sip of her drink.

I could tell it was a little painful for her to realize that she caused a lot of drama and I didn't want to make her feel any worse. "I'm sure it'll be old news by the end of the night." I stretched my hand out to rub her back. We sat in silence for a few moments and I proceeded to open my mouth to tell her that I had no hard feelings about what she did.

"Congrats on the new job, by the way," she said before I could get anything out.

"How did you know about that?" She either had immaculate hearing or she was a witch.

"I like to correct my mistakes." She took another sip of her drink and stared back out at the dance floor.

It was taking me a minute to really comprehend what she was telling me. It finally hit and I was a little speechless. I was wondering why Don had changed his mind about doing business with me, but I didn't think Janette had anything to do with it. I wanted to ask so many questions. What did she actually do? How did she persuade him to give me a better job than the one we previously discussed? Did she sleep with him? That last question got me a little uneasy and I thought it was best to just leave it alone. Knowing Janette, she'd found a way to convince him that I was worthy of this opportunity.

"Whatever you did, thank you."

"You don't have to thank me. Take it as my apology."

I wished I had the words to describe how I was feeling right now. I knew that Janette had her manipulative ways, but she'd never been a bad person. I appreciated the fact that she realized her mistake and fixed it. It meant a lot to me, especially since I got to have a better job out of the deal. I leaned over and kissed her on the cheek.

"Maybe you can come up to New York to visit me one weekend," I whispered in her ear.

Her eyes grew big and I could see her trying to contain her excitement. I wasn't sure if I really want to pursue an intimate relationship with Janette, but it didn't hurt to give her a chance. I grabbed her hand and led her to the dance floor. Now that I'd tied up all the loose ends, I was going to enjoy my last little moments in my hometown.

Chapter 36

Morgan

Lord knows this week had been one big rollercoaster, but I was so happy that it was about that time for Ahvi and me to go home. I missed everything about London: the vibe, the people, my own bed; I even missed the weather. Even though we had a ceremony, Ahvi and I were not legally married in Georgia so I planned on getting things legalized as soon as we got back home. I did appreciate my family getting over all the drama and supporting me. I actually had a good time yesterday. Nobody was tripping, everybody seemed to be enjoying themselves, and even though our reception was a part of the family banquet everyone still kept a focus on us. The funniest thing about yesterday was watching my aunt Wynona explain to Ahvi what Kool-Aid was. It took Ahvi ten minutes to grasp the concept that red was an actual flavor to black folks.

Ahvi and I stayed in the master suite at the manor. It was so nice to be back in her arms all night. Even though we weren't officially married, it definitely felt like we were.

I put the last item of clothing in our bag and zipped it up. We had to make two stops before we headed to the airport: to my parents' house to get the rest of our stuff and to the reading of my uncle's will. I had no idea what to expect at this thing, but the man hid the fact that I was his daughter for over twenty years. He might have been a millionaire as well.

"You ready, love?" Ahvi's voice echoed from the bathroom.

"You know, honey, maybe we should skip this whole thing and just head to the airport."

I sat back on the bed as Ahvi walked out of the bathroom. She took a seat next to me and stroked my back.

"Morgan, you have endured a lot this week, but I'm pretty sure the worst part is over."

I hated the fact that she was right. I was pretty sure all the tragic surprises had been uncovered, but I just didn't want to face the fact that Bug was my biological father. It was shocking to hear yesterday, but because there was so much going on it really hadn't sunk in. Going to this will reading felt like me driving head-first into a Mack Truck.

"Let's go deal with it and then we can go home."

Ahvi leaned over and kissed me on the lips. Without me giving her a response, she jumped off the bed and pulled me to the door. I guess I was going to face it whether I liked it or not.

I was quiet the whole ride over to the lawyer's office. I wanted to get my thoughts together and be completely prepared for anything. Every time Ahvi would inquire about something she saw or heard one of my family members say, I gave her brief answers. Now the walk into the building was becoming real. Ahvi and I appeared to be the last ones to arrive. Everyone was already in their seats, looking like they had been here for hours. My parents, my aunt, Janette, and JJ were sitting silently in front of the lawyer's desk.

"Sorry I'm late. We overslept." I took a seat and Ahvi scrambled behind me to find somewhere to sit.

"I'm sorry, ma'am. Who are you?" the lawyer said to Ahvi.

"Ahvianna Patel. I'm Morgan's spouse," she answered so proudly. It was so nice to hear those words.

"Legally?"

"Not here in the States, no."

"I'm sorry, but if you are not legally bonded then I can't allow you to stay."

I looked at Ahvi and nodded to her that it was okay to wait in the sitting area. I couldn't wait to get back home and fill out the appropriate papers because I never wanted this to happen again. The lawyer waited until Ahvi was out of the room before she continued.

"Welcome back, everyone. I know the last time we were here, things got a little uncomfortable."

I looked around the room to get an understanding on what she was talking about. I could only speculate that things hit the fan just like at the funeral.

"Is everyone okay today to proceed with the reading of the will?" The lawyer looked at each of us, waiting for a response.

"Yes," we all said in unison.

"Excellent, then we shall proceed."

My stomach was in knots. I didn't know why I was so nervous because I already knew he was my father. I guessed I was worried about what he could have for me. Whatever it was, I hoped he was just as generous to JJ and Janette. It was bad enough they had to find out I was their half sister; me getting more than them would not make it any better.

"First let me start by saying I am extremely sorry about your loss. I had the pleasure of working with Joe for a few years and he was a wonderful man." She took a breath and continued. "I, Joseph Lee Maxson Sr., of sound mind and body leave the following to my love ones after the conclusion of my life."

I could feel the butterflies in my stomach kick up. I glanced over at Janette and she seemed just as nervous as I was.

"To my lovely wife: thank you for always being by my side. I know there are things that you have discovered that are disheartening, but know that I have loved you since the first time I saw you until I took my last breath. I leave you the house, all my belongings, and my life savings you can find in the attic in a box marked 'green.' It should amount to a little over a hundred thousand dollars." The lawyer took a moment to give my aunt time to process what just was read to her.

My aunt flashed a sweet smile and I peeped a single tear fall down her face. I couldn't imagine what she was feeling at this moment, but I hoped this brought her a little peace.

"I wish I would have known that when I was burying him. He probably coulda got a nicer casket," my aunt joked. We all gave a little, uncomfortable chuckle and quickly recovered to allow the lawyer to keep reading.

"To my children JJ and Janette," she continued, "I have raised you from babies into well-functioning adults. I know I fell short sometimes as the father you needed, but know that I did everything because of you and your mother. I have set up a bank account for the both of you. I leave you fifty thousand dollars each. Spend it responsibly; especially you, Janette."

JJ and Nettie looked stunned. I couldn't tell if it was because of what he said or because he left them a substantial amount of money. I couldn't help but to wonder how Uncle Bug acquired all this money, but I remembered he played a lot of poker and bet on dogs and horses every week. My mother always said he had a lucky remedy. I guessed that was true.

"To my baby sister and brother-in-law," she continued, "words nor material things cannot express or amount to the gratitude I have for you both. You were my strength when I was weak. You allowed for not only my family, but yours as well, to function as a unit. I could have destroyed a lot of lives with my poor judgment and decisions, but you were the glue that kept everything together. I won a vacation home in Hawaii off of Troy Wilkes in 2009. I put the deed in your name last month. Thank you for being amazing parents to Morgan."

My mother burst into tears. I wasn't sure if they were happy or sad tears, but I thought it was a beautiful gesture of my uncle. My parents worked so hard without any down time; they deserved to take a break sometimes. A vacation home in Hawaii seemed like what they needed. My father wasn't a big fan of airplanes, but I thought he would make an exception for this.

"And last but not least, baby girl."

My stomach dropped to my feet when I heard my name. It seemed like everyone's eyes were on me.

"There are a lot of things that I need to explain to you. I can understand if you are angry with me, but know that I did my best to involve myself in your life. I'm leaving you an envelope that will help you further understand the circumstances by which you were conceived. Know that I love you with all my heart. You were a miracle to not only your parents but to me as well."

The lawyer closed the will and handed me a yellow envelope with the words "open in private" written on the front. I wasn't sure if I was grateful or upset to only be getting a packet. I was leaning toward grateful because I did need to know exactly who I was and what really happened. My parents were related to me and I knew they would always be a piece of me, but I needed to know the other half of me.

"That concludes the reading and execution of Joe Maxson's will. I know losing a loved one is tragic, but I hope this helps your healing." The lawyer gave us a polite smile and gestured toward the door for us to leave her office. "You all have a nice day."

We all quietly got up from our seats and filed out of her office one by one. When Ahvi and I saw each other in the waiting area, she popped up from her seat.

"What happened? What did he leave you?"

"I don't know yet." I flashed the envelope and Ahvi's face began to fill up with confusion. I grabbed her hand and told my family good-bye as we headed to the parking lot. I wanted to hurry up and get to a private place where I could see what he gave me. My parents stopped us before we got to the car.

"Are you okay about everything?" my mother asked as she gave me a hug.

"I don't know yet, Ma. But whatever is in here it doesn't change the fact that you guys are my parents." I glanced over to my father and noticed he was trying to hold back tears. It was the first time this whole week I saw him letting out some emotion.

"We brought your stuff. We didn't know how long this would take and we didn't want y'all to miss your flight," he said, trying to change the subject before a tear fell.

Ahvi went to retrieve our bags and my parents and I had our final moment together.

"You guys try to go to that vacation home at least twice a year please." I didn't think saying good-bye to my parents was going to be this hard, but it was. I was becoming emotional.

"We'll try," Mama said through her tears that were beginning to fall.

Without another word I fell into my mother's arms and I immediately felt my father join in on the hug. We never did a group hug, but this felt so appropriate.

"I love you guys," I was able to whisper.

"We love you too," they said in unison.

We finally let go of our embrace and I took my last look at the people who raised me. I didn't think I could have had better parents, even if I had picked them. Ahvi and I said our last good-byes and got in the car.

I let her drive because we both wanted to see what was in the envelope. As soon as we were safely on the highway, I ripped the thing open like a Christmas present. A bunch of pictures and documents fell out of it. I noticed a folded-up letter and opened it.

My Dearest Morgan,

If you are reading this than you have found out that I am your biological father. I first want to apologize for keeping such a big secret from you, but I did it for your own good. You deserved the type of parents Beanie and Earl are to you. Your birth mother's name was Norma Rae Lewis. She was a runaway from Chicago and I met her in Atlanta. She had such a beautiful spirit for someone who went through as much as she did. You remind me of her sometimes. My marriage was in a rocky stage and I gravitated toward Norma Rae. I genuinely cared a lot about her and at one point I could see myself with her forever. It wasn't until I patched things up with your aunt that I found out Norma Rae was pregnant with you. I wasn't there for her, so when I got the phone call that she had passed due to complications during childbirth, I needed to make sure you were taken care of. Beanie and Earl had just lost a son and I knew they would give you all the love you could handle and more. I tried to do as much as I could as your uncle. You have always been so precious to me and I hope one day you can find it in your heart to forgive me for betraying your trust. I have enclosed a few pictures of your birth mother so you know what she looks like. All you really have to do is look in the mirror because you are a spitting image of her. There is also a bank card for an account I opened up the day I gave you to Beanie. It has a little over fifty thousand dollars in it. I love you with all my heart, my beautiful daughter.

    Sincerely,
    Your Bug

Water was just dripping down my face onto the letter. I couldn't stop myself from crying. I was overwhelmed with emotions. It was a shock when Janette blurted it out and my parents confirmed it, but reading it from Uncle Bug was sad and beautiful at the same time.

I wiped my face and picked up a picture of Norma Rae. She was gorgeous. She had big, curly shoulder-length hair, a Coke-bottle shape, beautiful caramel skin, and big, pouty lips. She was a vision and I did look just like her. She had a smile on her face in the picture but I could tell behind her eyes she was a tortured soul. I could see she had been through a lot in her short life.

I picked up another picture of her while she was big and pregnant. I flipped it over and there was writing on the back of it:

"Seven months pregnant with the most beautiful gift I've ever received. My baby girl."

I tried to hold it back but I began to weep uncontrollably. I was so grateful to Uncle Bug for giving me this beautiful gift: to know of her. There was no way I could be upset about the circumstances. At the end of the day I knew I was loved unconditionally, and that was really all that mattered.